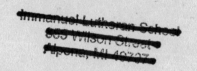

The Funeral Director's Son

The Funeral Director's Son

Coleen Murtagh Paratore

Simon & Schuster Books for Young Readers
New York London Toronto Sydney

SIMON & SCHUSTER BOOKS FOR YOUNG READERS
An imprint of Simon & Schuster Children's Publishing Division
1230 Avenue of the Americas, New York, New York 10020

This book is a work of fiction. Any references to historical events, real people, or real locales are used fictitiously. Other names, characters, places, and incidents are the product of the author's imagination, and any resemblance to actual events or locales or persons, living or dead, is entirely coincidental.

Text copyright © 2008 by Coleen Murtagh Paratore
All rights reserved, including the right of reproduction in whole or in part in any form.
SIMON & SCHUSTER BOOKS FOR YOUNG READERS is a trademark of Simon & Schuster, Inc.
For information about special discounts for bulk purchases, please contact Simon & Schuster Special Sales at 1-866-506-1949 or business@simonandschuster.com.
The Simon & Schuster Speakers Bureau can bring authors to your live event. For more information or to book an event, contact the Simon & Schuster Speakers Bureau at 1-866-248-3049 or visit our website at www.simonspeakers.com.
Also available in a Simon and Schuster Books for Young Readers hardcover edition.
Book design by Karen Hudson
The text of this book was set in Berkeley.
Manufactured in the United States of America
First Simon & Schuster Books for Young Readers paperback edition August 2009
2 4 6 8 10 9 7 5 3 1
The Library of Congress has cataloged the hardcover edition as follows:
Paratore, Coleen
The funeral director's son/Coleen Murtagh Paratore—1st ed.
134 p; 18 cm
Summary: The last thing twelve-year-old Christopher "Kip" Campbell wants is to take over the funeral business that has been in his family for generations, but he is the only Campbell heir and seems to have a calling to help the dead and their survivors in a most unusual way.
ISBN-13: 978-1-4169-3594-0 (hc)
[1.Undertakers and undertaking—Fiction. 2. Funeral homes—Fiction. 3. Dead—Fiction. 4. Family-owned business enterprises—Fiction. 5. Family life—Massachusetts—Fiction. 6. Massachusetts—Fiction]
PZ7.P2137 Fu 2008
[Fic]—22
2007028696
ISBN: 978-1-4169-3595-7 (pbk)
ISBN: 978-1-4169-8276-0 (eBook)

To my son, Christopher,

who once won a contest predicting

what a certain "new year" would bring.

Thankfully, all predictions continue to come true,

year, after year, after glorious green year.

With love and admiration,

Mom

As printed in the *Times Union*, Albany, New York,

January 16, 1996:

"A Green Scene"

by Christopher Paratore, age 6

First grade, Guilderland Elementary School

In the new year . . .

I think flowers will grow.

The snow will melt.

The trees will have leaves.

Grass will be green.

And kids will start playing outside.

Contents

CHAPTER 1

Campbell and Sons

There are only two styles of portrait painting;
the serious and the smirk . . .

—Charles Dickens, *Nicholas Nickleby*

I spend a lot of time thinking about *f*-words.

Food. Friends. Fun.

And funerals.

That's right, funerals. Our family runs Campbell and Sons Funeral Home. We live upstairs from the business. Family on the second floor. Funerals on the first. Frankenstein stuff in the basement. When you kick it in Clover, my home is your home. You're welcome anytime. Every day that ends in *y*. Morning, noon, or night.

It's been that way since 1875. Ever since my great-great-great-great-grandfather Christopher Adams Campbell had the fishbrain idea to start a funeral business. He was a carpenter, the only one in town, and I guess he was building so many caskets, he figured he might as well bury them too.

I wish the old Pilgrim could have picked a better product. Potato chips or bubble gum or chicken soup or something. But that's spit off Clover Cliff at this point. As we say in the funeral field, we're in it "forever" now.

For six long generations, Campbell and Sons Funeral Home has been proudly, and I mean *proudly*, passed on down from Campbell father to son . . . to son . . . to son. And that's fine if you like hanging around dead people. I don't.

That's a problem. A big one. Because unless one of my sisters grows a mustache and crosses over, there's only one Campbell son in this entire generation.

Me.

And every time I pass by that long line of Christophers hanging on the wall in the hall downstairs—the gold-trimmed ghostly-grim faces of every Christopher Campbell, Funeral Director, from Christopher Adams Campbell to Christopher Bartholomew Campbell to Christopher Clemson Campbell . . . all the way to my father, Christopher

Francis Campbell—a snaky shiver runs down my spine.

And when I come to the end of the line and see that space on the wall next to my Dad. The perfect-size spot for one more portrait. The place where my face is supposed to go. I get a punch-in-the-gut-puke-it-up feeling.

All I can think about is: how can I stop history?

How can I be the first Christopher to break the family curse?

Be a Christopher Columbus, not a Christopher Campbell.

Chart a new course, pull up anchor, catch the wind, and sail away.

Even though, I know, it will break my father's heart.

CHAPTER 2

Everybody Pitches In

Oh let us love our occupations,
Bless the squire and his relations,
Live upon our daily rations,
And always know our proper stations.

—Charles Dickens, *The Chimes*

"We're a family business, a team," Mom says. "Everybody pitches in."

Mom's not talking baseball. She's talking work. We all have a job.

Abraham Banfield's wake is tonight. He's laid out in the parlor. Spiffy gray suit, gold pocket watch, a hat with a feather on the brim. Abe was the richest man in Clover. Owned the paper mill and printing plant where half the town worked, until he shut them down, no warning. Hung a sign on the gate. *Closed.* A hundred people lost their jobs. That hit hard. Clover might have been lucky once, but it sure isn't lucky now.

"Selfish old son of a witch," my grandmother, Nanbull, said when Abe closed the mill. Nanbull calls it true as she sees it, no tiptoeing around, making nice.

After school, I go to check on Abe. The parlor's all set for the viewing. Chairs lined in perfect rows, purple drapes, lights low. Everything normal, except there's no flowers. Who would send them? Everybody hated him. Money can't buy you friends.

My hand glides smooth along the coffin, mahogany and brass. This box cost as much as a car. Huge waste of money if you ask me. One night's show, then in the ground forever. Only the best for Banfield, though. He arranged his funeral and paid Dad ahead. "Cadillac casket," no music, no preacher, Banfield vault, *done.*

I stare down at the dead man's face, not feeling a smidgeon of sadness. Won't need buckets for the tears tonight. I'll be surprised if anyone shows. Too bad, because Uncle Marty did a good job prepping Abe. Puffed up his cheeks, which were all sunk in from the cancer, and pumped in a nice Florida glow.

Uncle Marty is our Embalmer. He does the mad science in the Frankenstein lab in the basement. We don't really call it the Frankenstein lab. That's an inside joke.

Inside my head, that is. Dad would be mad if he heard. He'd say it was disrespectful.

Uncle Marty scrubs up like a surgeon in an operating room, handling all the instruments and solutions to prepare a body for viewing. Sort of a doctor of deadology. It's important work. He gives families one final nice look at the person they loved.

I can't imagine losing someone I love. I was a baby when Gramp went. I don't remember him. I know lots of people who've died, though. Most every call we handle. Clover is a small town and we're the only funeral home. Well, we used to be.

And I'm usually okay unless somebody cracks. There'll be all these people dressed in black, standing around mumbling "sorry for your loss" . . . "such a good man" . . . "suffering's over" . . . "loved you so much" . . . whispering memories soft and low, like bumblebees humming. Then all of a sudden, a cry cuts through or a yelp like a hunting dog caught in a trap, and my gut caves in. *What if Nanbull died . . . or Mom . . . or Dad . . .*

"How was school, Kip?" Dad says, coming to stand by me. Kip's my nickname. Dad's got one too. His friends at the Elks Lodge call him "Boss." I'm not sure why. He's not bossy at all. My sister Lizbreath's got that job locked. Maybe it's because Dad's the biggest guy in Clover, seven feet high and fat as Santa. Buys his suits at the Big and Tall Men store. Dad hasn't bought new clothes in a while though. None of us have. Business has been slow. Abe Banfield's the first call we've had in a month.

Dad and I stare down at Abe. "He looks good," I say.

"Uncle Marty's a master," Dad says, nodding. "Abe was skin, bones, and liver spots. Bet that embalmer at Golden's can't restore like this."

Golden's Funeral Home just opened this year, and they're already hurting us. Part of a national chain. Nanbull calls them the "cowboys." Four viewing rooms, huge chapel. TV commercials every night comparing their prices to Campbell's. It's like when PriceCheck came to Clover and killed Miller's SuperMarket. Mr. Miller couldn't compete. People in town stayed loyal for a while, but in the end, money talked. I see Dad shaking his head reading the obituary page in the morning, all the calls we're losing to Golden's, more sad than mad. Dad knows every one of those families.

"I'm worried about Fred," Dad says. Fred is Abe Banfield's son. "He'll regret it forever if he doesn't come home. One last chance to see his father. Heal that wound."

Everybody in Clover knows the story. Our family was there. A few years back, Easter Sunday, at the Clover Inn. Fred brought home a girl. They were engaged. Abe didn't approve. Shanisse wasn't the "right color" or the "right religion." Worst of all for Abe, she wasn't rich. Abe called her a "gold digger." He shouted "gold digger," his face tomato red, right out loud in the restaurant. Abe said he'd cut Fred out of his will if he married "that girl."

Fred and Shanisse left town that day and never came back. Mom heard they got married, bought a house in Boston, had a baby boy.

"I wouldn't count on Fred coming," I say.

"You're probably right, son. I've been trying to reach him since the death, hoping he'd get involved in the arrangements, but no."

Dad is our Arranger. He helps families plan

funerals, but mostly he helps them cope. Dad says, "Funerals are for the living. The dead we don't have to worry about."

Dad doesn't know it, but that's not always true.

When Dad does an arrangement session, it's like he's going to church. He puts on one of his funeral director suits and greets the family at the door. No one is allowed to interrupt. No phone calls, beepers, buzzers. Even Mosely knows better than to *meow*.

Dad sits patiently, passing out tissues, doling out Boss Campbell bear hugs if the families are huggers or just nodding nicely if they aren't, listening with his big Boss Campbell ears and big brown Boss Campbell eyes, comforting and sympathetic.

People feel better when my dad is around. He lets them talk and cry as long as they need. "Never rush grief," he says. And he doesn't try selling them expensive caskets and vaults. We'd be a lot richer if he did. No, Dad is an old-fashioned family-first funeral director. "One of a dying breed," Nanbull says.

Dying breed, get it?

Dad says funeral service isn't a business, it's a calling. Maybe so, but I'm not answering. When they try hanging me on the wall, the only calling I'm doing is quits.

"Final check," Aunt Sally says, bustling in with her case. She fixes Abe's hair. Aunt Sal and Uncle Marty live next door with their tabbies, Winken, Blinken, and Nod.

Aunt Sally is our Cosmetician. Hair and makeup. Personally I think she went too red on Miss Platt's lipstick, and giving Mr. Burg a black toupee when he was a baldie seemed wrong, but what do I know? I don't wear makeup, and who cares about hair.

My mother comes in. "Still no flowers?" She shakes her head and hurries off. Mom, Evelyn Campbell, is our Manager. She runs the office, pays the bills, and works every wake with my dad. People say Mom has the biggest heart in Clover. She even gives hearts away. After the burial at Willow Grove, Mom gives the family a *Dicentra spectabilis*. A bleeding heart plant. "For your garden," she whispers with a smile.

The flowers are shaped like little pink hearts. They bloom again every spring. Perennial. Mom says, "The people you love live on in your heart forever."

Mom returns with a vase of yellow flowers. "Just picked these mums this afternoon." She sets them by the head of the coffin. "There you go, Abe, that's better." My mom is so nice. One time Dad heard me teasing her for sprinkling coffee grinds on her flower beds. He took me aside and said, "If your mother thinks piss'll help her petunias, you start whizzing in the garden, you hear me?"

No problem there, I told my dad. I like a good whiz in the wind.

Nanbull comes in wearing a red dress. She smiles at me and opens the register book that Abe's guests will sign. Nanbull is our Writer. She does the obituaries, memorial cards, and funeral programs. Lizbreath named her "Nanbull" when she was little, and Nanbull liked it, I guess because it didn't peg her as a granny. Actually, "Nanbull" suits her. She's tiny, but tough as a bull.

Mom says Nanbull has a "potty mouth." Mom has a jar in the kitchen, and when Nanbull swears, Mom makes her put in a quarter. "Please, Nora, the children."

Nanbull rolls her eyes. "Words are words, Evelyn. Some just have more sizzle."

Lately, Nanbull has been doing almost-swears. Like "holy ship" and "what the shell." She cracks me up. And Nanbull is really good at her job. She writes an obituary like a story. "Tell readers Mary Dodge was a 'good neighbor' and they'll forget, Kip. Tell them 'Mary made fresh strawberry shortcake every

June and delivered plates warm with whipped cream on top to all of her friends on Stowe Avenue' . . . and that they'll remember."

Nanbull's sister, Great-aunt Aggie, is our Musician. She has the night off from the organ since Abe specified "no music." Aunt Aggie wears dresses buttoned tight to her chin, white hair in a doughnut on her head. For fun she knits "ladies in waiting." Mouse ladies in ruffly gowns you can cover spare rolls of toilet paper with. Aunt Aggie sells them at St. Mary's summer carnival and the Christmas bazaar. The ladies carry signs:

IF YOU SPRINKLE WHEN YOU TINKLE,
PLEASE BE NEAT AND WIPE THE SEAT.

Aunt Aggie sort of looks like her mouse ladies. She's even got some whiskers.

Nanbull rolls her eyes about Aunt Aggie's mouse ladies. And Aunt Aggie rolls her eyes about Nanbull's swears. "Please try to be a lady, Nora," Aunt Aggie huffs.

"I am a lady," Nanbull says, "but I sure the heck ain't a mouse."

Nanbull never remarried after Gramp died, but

she's had some nice boyfriends. Right now it's Sal Delicato. He runs Sal's Sips and Subs on Front Street. Sal gives me free chocolate shakes and meatball subs, I think maybe so I'll tell Nanbull to marry him.

I figure I've got Sal Delicato in a really good spot. Keep the subs coming, Sal.

"Dinner's ready," Mom says.

I head upstairs to our floor. Lizbreath's in the kitchen eating a sandwich. When we have a call in, it's a sandwich night. Can't have cooking smells floating downstairs during a viewing. No running, no noise, no nothing.

"Hurry up and eat," Lizbreath says. "And change your clothes. And don't forget to sweep the stoop and put out the parking cones."

Lizbreath is sixteen, four years older than me. Her real name's Elizabeth, but she changed it to Lizbeth in high school. "Practice it, Kip," she says. "*Liz-Beth.* Accent on the *first* syllable."

I call her Liz-*breath* because she's always breathing in my face, bossing me around.

Lizbreath's job is Florist. Plucking dead-heads off the arrangements and picking up petals from the floor. Lizbreath has bigger plans, though. She wants to run the showroom where the caskets and urns are displayed. She says we need a "merchandising makeover." We "need to put some FUN in *funeral*." Call the showroom "the Salon." Offer customers "a more pleasant shopping experience." Crystal glasses of sherry and finger sandwiches, mannequins displaying funeral gowns and jewelry, crowns even.

"The dead should be laid to rest royally, like the ancient Egyptians," Lizbreath says, "and we could charge a ton more that way, too."

Dad listens patiently, like he respects her opinion. Except for the making more money part, I think Lizbreath's a fishbrain. She wants to go to Paris to study fashion in college. I'd miss her so much. *Yeah, right.*

"Kip!" My little sister Chick runs to hug me, red clown curls, big blue eyes, a sheet of smiley stickers in her hand. Chick's three. Her real name is Chastity, some old family name, poor kid, but we all call her Chick. She'll thank us for that someday.

Chick's official job is Giggler. She thinks it's a big birthday party having all these people downstairs. She doesn't even realize the one in the coffin is cold. Chick runs around giggling, trying to put smiley stickers on people's faces. "Do you want a red one, a blue one, a green, or a yellow?" She has the funniest little laugh. It's contagious. When you hear Chick giggle, you smile too. Not a bad thing in a funeral home.

Bzzzzzzzzzzz. Dad rings the antique buzzer. We all know the drill. Get to our stations. Ten minutes to showtime. I button my shirt, slip on my tie and blazer.

Downstairs, I sweep the front steps, brush a few leaves off the walkway. I put Mosely on his leash and take my spot in the parking lot. At Campbell and Sons, we all have a job. Officially I'm the Outdoor Guy. I sweep, mow, rake, and shovel, and I direct parking during calling hours. But I also have a secret job.

I help the dead rest in peace.

CHAPTER 3

Outdoor Guy

*Pause you who read this, and think for a moment
of the long chain of iron or gold… that would never
have bound you, but for the formation of the first
link on one memorable day.*

—Charles Dickens, *Great Expectations*

It's chilly out here in the parking lot, cold for October. Nobody's showing up for Abe's wake. I set out the Funeral Parking cones and sit on my stool to wait for cars. "Outdoor Guy" suits me fine. No smelly carnations or people crying or dead bodies.

Not anymore, but when I was little, I thought dead people might be contagious. Maybe you could catch "dead" like the chicken pox. I held my breath when I ran downstairs and out the front door to school in the morning, and I wouldn't breathe until I reached the corner where Tuck, Jupey, and Stew were waiting. They're still my best friends. We still meet at the corner.

Anyway, so my family calls me the Outdoor Guy. They don't know my other job. Most of the time, my work is boring, like Clark Kent or Bruce Wayne or Peter Parker. Then once in a while, things get interesting. No cool cape or bat cave or web stuff. And I don't get paid a cent. But that's changing or I'm quitting. I'm done helping the dead. Sometimes I almost tell Nanbull. I think maybe she knows about my other job. One time she said I had "a gift." But a gift should make you happy, right?

It all started one summer day when I was sitting out on my throne thinking, and I heard a voice in my head. There's this secret spot on Clover Cliff only I know about. It's like a chair carved into the rocks way up above the water. You have to crawl out over the sea wall to get there. It's high up and dangerous. Fun. Bird's-eye view of the beach and ocean. Neptune, king of the sea. I sit there imagining what the world's like out beyond the horizon line, all the places I'm headed when I sail out of here.

When your family runs a funeral home, you don't get away much. No Disney or Grand Canyon. Not even a mountain camp with your friends. Over the bridge to Cape Cod is as far as I've been. You never know when a family will need us.

"We Campbells are here to serve," Dad says. "It is a sacred pact, an honor. Our families depend on us all year long. Every day that ends in y. Morning, noon, or night."

Well, I don't know if it will be morning, noon, or night, but as soon as I can, I'm leaving. Red rover, red rover, see ya later, Clover. Tuck, Jupe, and Stew are coming too. We're off to the good life. Fun and adventure. Jungles, deserts, amusement parks. Eat when we want, sleep when we want, explore all the continents, see the Seven Wonders of the World, or the Eight or Nine, however many there are. That's what we're going to do.

The Frankenstein lab never interested me. Arranging doesn't either. When Dad consoles a man who lost his wife, or a lady who lost her baby, all I want to do is bolt. Paying bills is boring. I don't like flowers or selling stuff. Hair and makeup are dumb. I don't giggle. I'm not musical. Obituaries are out. I hate to write—too many rules.

I know Dad's worried I won't carry on the Campbell legacy. When I turned twelve, that seemed to be a magic number. He started asking if

I'd like to learn more about the business, become his "apprentice," go to the Massachusetts Funeral Convention in Springfield with him. Good thing my baseball team made the finals and I got out of it.

Dad knew I was relieved. He knows I don't have the calling, and he's concerned.

I heard Mom say, "Give him time, Chris. Let him spread his wings a bit, go to Camp Russell this summer." That's the Adirondack camp Stew and Jupe go to for two weeks every year. Dad says it's too far and too expensive. Tuck can't afford it either.

I overhear Mom and Dad talking a lot. My ears are like satellite dishes. I can pick up shows in seven languages. My ears are so big I can hang my backpack on the left one and my gym bag on the right. So big I can hear voices nobody else can . . . *Meoow.* Mosely rubs against my leg. "Hey, buddy." I scratch him under the chin.

Mose is a pretty good dog for a cat. My whole life I wanted a dog, but when you live in a funeral home, you can't risk barking during calling hours. I'm lucky I got a cat. Dad always said, "no pets, no pets," but one day Nanbull and I were walking by Wayshak's pet store. It was cat-adoption day. The minute I saw him, I knew he was mine. Shiny black coat, white paws and chest. "A tuxedo cat," Mr. Wayshak said. The cat's tag said "Michael."

"Michael?" Nanbull said, rolling her eyes. "What kind of name is that? He looks like that Puss and Boots cat. You're his human now, Kip. Give him a decent name."

I think she was rooting for Puss or Boots. I scratched the cat's head. He had a wet nose. "How about Mose?" I said, "Mosely?"

"Nice." Nanbull nodded. "I like it."

Finally, a car pulls in for Abe's wake. Father Tallman. He probably felt spiritually obligated.

"Evening, Kip," he says.

"Evening, Father."

"Nice night," he says.

"Sure is, Father." I'm hoping he doesn't mention last Sunday. Tuck and I were flinging holy water and we baptized Mrs. Divitt by mistake. She wasn't pleased.

Doc Burton pulls in next. Bet he felt guilted into coming too.

"How's the foot, Kip," he asks.

I just got the cast off from when I dropped a bowling ball. "Good, sir," I say.

A half hour goes by, nobody. Then the Birdlady

makes her appearance. Kids call her that because she's always got birds around her. She never misses a wake. She passes me, head down, without a word, the hood of her coat drawn around her face. When she gets inside, she'll kneel by the coffin, make the sign of the cross, sniff the flowers, take a prayer card, then hightail out before Lizbreath scolds her.

Dad always says, "Leave her be, Lizbeth. She's just a bit off, that's all. Every town's got a woodle. She's ours." *Woodle* is about as close as Dad gets to a swear.

Another hour goes by. It's getting dark. Poor Abe. Richest guy in town, you'd figure more than three people would show up to say "Nice job, see ya later." I gather the cones—didn't need these tonight—and turn around smack into Billy Blye.

Ahhh, I suck in air like a vacuum. After all these years, he still spooks me.

"Outta me way," Blye grumbles. He spits and squints his good eye at me. I see the spot where the other eye was. Looks like he sewed it himself. Crazy, mean old fisherman. Probably opened his tackle box, pulled out a hook and line. Figures Blye would come to Abe's wake. Cut from the same mean sailcloth, those two.

I think about the summer I turned six. I was on the beach sailing the new kite Dad got me for my birthday. It was a beaut. A huge silvery bird. It glittered so bright my eyes burned as I watched it soar higher and higher.

But then the wind quit, and the bird fell on Blye's property. On the gray spiked fence, covered with wild pink beach roses, rugosa they're called. I pricked my fingers on the thorns trying to get my kite untangled. I heard a man shout, "Get on from there!" I worked faster, trying to set the kite free. "Get on from there," the voice boomed again. I heard a door open, boots stomping on the porch, and then a hand yanked me up gruffly by the back of my neck and dropped me down on the road. "Stay away from me roses or I'll trap ya like a lobsta and boil ya till ya scream."

I screamed all right and ran home crying. When I went back the next day, my kite was gone.

Prrr-rrr-rrr, Mosely is growling strangely.

I look at my watch. Calling hours are over. I've got homework. "Come on, Mose." I tug on his leash. Poor cat has to wear it, or there could be trouble. When we first got him, we had a cremation call in. Mrs. Ashanti. I heard a crash at night and went downstairs. Mosely was in the parlor, looking like a ghost cat all covered in white. White ashes. Mrs. Ashanti's ashes. I swept her up quick and got a new urn from the showroom but Dad figured it out. Dad said we could have gotten sued, closed down even.

Then a week later Mosely snuck downstairs during Mr. Pizola's wake, on the prowl for something. Right when Mrs. Pizola went to kiss her husband good night, Mose popped his head out of the coffin with a mouse in his mouth. Mrs. Pizola screamed bloody murder—nearly croaked herself. Not the reaction Mose was hoping for. He was proud of his catch. Now it's the leash or nothing. Poor Mose. All spiffy in his tux, cool cat on the town, and we leash him like a poodle. It's embarrassing. I swear his face gets red. "What's black and white and red all over?" It's Mosely on his leash.

"Come on, boy." Mose pulls away, purring up at the sky. Odd, since he's not much of a stargazer. Mosely's a land man, nose to the ground, sniffing for slow stuff.

"Come on, Mose, now."

Mosely keeps staring up, ears pointed like arrows.

I look up too. Millions of stars and a sugar cookie moon.

Then I see it.

A ship. Well, stars in the shape of a ship. There's the mast and the mainsail.

A foghorn bellows loud and clear, like the ferry heading out to the Vineyard. Except the sound isn't coming from the docks; it's coming from the sky. The horn *boooooooms* again, louder and longer. Mosely and I watch, not blinking.

It's quiet. Stone quiet. So quiet I can hear the stars shine.

Abe's heart is too heavy, Kip. Help him loosen that anchor so he can board.

CHAPTER 4

Abe's Anchor

"I wear the chain I forged in life . . ."

—Charles Dickens, *A Christmas Carol*

Abe Banfield was an easy case. I knew what was weighing him down. Doc Burton told Dad at the wake, but I guessed it, anyway.

For all Abe's power and fortune, in his final hours at Clover Hospital, old Abe had one simple wish. To tell his son, Fred, something.

But Fred didn't come.

When Abe Banfield died, he was skinny as a skeleton. His heart was a heavier matter. The enormous weight of regret he felt for how badly he had treated his only son pinned Abe down like an anchor, a Moby Dick–size anchor with a cast-iron chain.

When the ship came, Abe couldn't go.

You have to be light as a kite to sail.

It was easy tracking down Fred Banfield. It helps that my friend Jupey's father is a cop. It took half my savings to get to Boston, though. Nanbull was my accomplice. She trusted me that it was important and didn't ask a ton of questions.

We snuck Gramp Campbell's antique hearse out of the garage. Nanbull drove. I paid for the gas. Who knew gas was so expensive? And tolls. And parking. And burgers to go. Nanbull doesn't have extra money. I insisted on paying for everything.

Nanbull wore her big red hat, black sunglasses, and a yellow scarf that whipped out the window like a flag. Nanbull loves dressing like a movie star. People stared and waved. We stopped traffic in Beantown. I think they really thought we were stars.

We followed the directions to Fred Banfield's school. He teaches sixth-grade social studies. Nanbull waited outside. Fred was in his classroom, writing something on the board. "May I help you?" he asked.

"I'm Kip Campbell. From Clover. Your father sent me."

"My father's dead," he said, looking spooked, sitting down in his teacher chair.

"I know. But he can't move on yet. He needs me to tell you something."

Fred rolled backward. His chair hit the chalkboard. "What are you—an angel?"

"Yeah, right," I laughed. "I'm no angel. Believe me. Your dad just needs to tell you something before he can sail. Something important. I think you'll want to hear it."

I felt sorry for Fred then. His face scrunched up like a baby with gas. He made a squeaking sound and started bawling before I even said the message:

"I'm sorry, son, and I love you."

CHAPTER 5

"Gold"

Dumb as a drum with a hole in it, sir…

—Charles Dickens, *Pickwick Papers*

There's a shamrock on the "Welcome to Clover" sign when you come in to our town. Three round green leaves on a short fat stem. Nanbull says the three petals remind us why we're here. "To live. To love. To leave something better behind."

Three simple things to get yourself a spot in heaven.

It sounds easy, but you'd be surprised how people can screw things up. Most everyone who dies in Clover moves on without help from me. They live, they love, they leave something better behind. And so, when the ship comes, they're ready to go to good.

That's what I think heaven is. Good.

But other people have trouble leaving. Anchors

weigh them down. Something they didn't say. Something they didn't do. That's where I come in.

I've been helping the dead for a while now, but I made up my mind, I'm quitting. I need a job that pays money. Lots of it. There aren't any good jobs in Clover anymore. Not since Banfield shut the mill. Not since Clover Chips closed. Not since the new bridge that takes the tourists straight over Clover and out to Cape Cod. "Now we're the ugly troll that lives under the bridge," Nanbull says. "What we need is some leprechaun luck."

Well, I don't know any leprechauns. All I know is Clover's dying and the Campbells are broke. I want money to go to Camp Russell. A computer like the rest of the planet. A new bike. Sneakers somebody's heard of. But most of all, I need to save for my boat.

Nauset Whalers don't come cheap.

Jupey, Stew, Tuck, and I have been working on schemes to make money. Nanbull says we've got "entrepreneurial talent." I thought our Sun Runners idea would be a gold mine, but we didn't even clear a hundred bucks running to the snack bar for people on Carey's Beach all summer. We sweated like pigs running up and down the stairs, and all we got were quarters here and there. Made me want to spill some sodas on purpose.

And we sure aren't buying a Whaler on Jupey's county-fair contests. Pies and hotdogs just don't pay, no matter how many you stuff in. Some of the new contests Jupe found sound promising. The lawnmower race in Lee, and the dress-your-pet-as-a-lobster in Plymouth. I'm fast on a John Deere, and Mosely looks good in red. We've got potential with those. But that's still chump change. I need a real job. Big bucks. I'm giving my notice today. I'm done with the dead. Let somebody else help them.

After school I bike to Clover Cliff, crawl out across the rocks to my throne. The wind whistles loudly in my ears. The first time I heard a voice, that's what I thought it was. The wind. But then I heard words, real words. *Tell Mrs. Burton not to worry about Doc. He'll miss her, but he'll be fine. Tell Molly the ship is waiting, Kip. It's time to go to good.* What! I jumped when I heard that voice, nearly fell into the ocean. I looked around—nobody there. Weird.

That night Nanbull asked me to go to Doc Burton's house with her. This wasn't unusual. She and Mrs. Burton were good friends. We picked up a vanilla shake at Sal's on the way. "Molly's too sick to eat, Kip, but maybe she'll enjoy this."

While we were visiting, Nanbull went to the kitchen for something and I was alone with Mrs. Burton. She moaned in pain, then looked at me. I held her bony hand. "Doc will be fine, Mrs. Burton. It's okay. The ship is waiting. Go to good now. It's all right."

Mrs. Burton closed her eyes and smiled. She looked so peaceful. She died that night. Doc Burton was sad, but relieved that his wife was finally out of pain. I have to admit, it felt good to have helped her, but . . . "No," I shout at the waves. "I'm done. I don't want to do this anymore. Do you hear me? I need to get a job that pays. Real money. Do you hear me?"

I close my eyes and listen hard. Nothing.

I hear someone calling up from the beach. I look down.

Caw-caw. Just a seagull and the Birdlady. The strange old woman stares up at me. Our eyes meet for a second.

Caw-caw, the gull squawks and rises up, then settles on the Birdlady's shoulder. She turns and walks off, a yellow PriceCheck bag in each hand. She stops, picks up a can, shake-shake-shakes it, puts it in a bag. A few yards later, she bends to pick up something else. She turns back to look up at me, holding something out in the palm of her hand. It sparkles in the sun. She throws it on the sand and hurries off. Weird.

I crawl back over the sea wall to the top of the beach stairs. Bub Jeffers and Dirk Hogan are by the railing, doing something to my bike. They move away when they see me. "This thing even work, Deadbo?" Bub says.

Bub made up the name "Deadbo." Combined my family's business with my Dumbo ears. Probably the cleverest thing Bub ever came up with. Maybe the only thing. He's "dumb as a drum with a hole in it," as Nanbull would say.

"Deadbo doesn't need a bike," Dirk says. "All he has to do is flap those ears and he can fly anywhere." He waves his arms in the air to demonstrate.

Dirk-the-jerk is Bub's best friend. They are the biggest guys in our seventh-grade class. They look like they ought to be in high school. Probably flunked kindergarten twice or something. Probably couldn't sing the ABCs or tie their shoes or something.

"Good one, Dirk," Bub says, flapping his arms too.

Back in fourth grade, I actually tried to be friends with them. We were on the same basketball team.

We all sucked up to Bub because his father was the coach, figured we'd get more court time. Everybody used to do sleepovers after the games. I kept inviting kids to my house, but they always said no. One night in the locker room, I overheard why. "Remember," Bub said, laugh-snorting so hard he could barely finish, "don't ever sleep over at Campbell's house or you'll never wake up again."

That night was a wake-up call for me. Before that, nobody cared what my dad did for a living. But all of a sudden it was freaking people out. After that, if somebody said, "Aren't you the funeral director's son?" I'd say, "No, not me."

"C'mon," Bub says, "we're late for practice."

"Later, Deadbo," Dirk says.

They take off laughing. I watch them, fists clenched. Get a grip, Kip. I stare at the waves, my fists clenched, my eyes stinging.

Do this work for one more year and it will be worth your weight in gold.

The voice rings loud above the crash of the waves.

Gold? What good is gold? This isn't pirate times. What am I going to do . . . walk down to Maloney's Marina, dump a sack of coins on the counter and say

"Hey, mister, can you count these up and see if I have enough for that nice Nauset Whaler?"

The wind whips against my face. I stand there, ears wide open, but there is nothing more. I throw a rock, then another, and another. Gold? Yeah, right. Of all the dumb, fishbrain ideas.

CHAPTER 6

It's a Deal

"As good as gold . . ."

—Charles Dickens, *A Christmas Carol*

Gold? Worth my weight in gold. What's that supposed to mean? Nobody buys stuff with gold anymore. I bike home grumbling mad.

Campbell and Sons is on the corner of Piper and Glenn. Tall, redbrick, green canvas awnings on the windows, black iron fence all around. One of the biggest, oldest houses in Clover. It might have been nice long ago. It needs embalming now. Stuff is crumbling, cracking, corroding. Needs a new roof, new chimney, new sidewalk. And that's just the outside. The state is going to shut us down if we don't "meet codes" by the end of the year. New wiring and ventilation. Handicap access. Tons of codes. Expensive codes. I overhear Mom and Dad in the kitchen, whispering so they won't worry us, but I've got satellite ears. I feel bad for Dad, but I can't help hoping. Those codes might be my lucky break. The codes or the cowboys. Either way, we're in trouble.

Worth your weight in gold, my gut. I'm still fuming when I reach our floor. You think I'm going to bite on that? Of all the dumb, fishbrain . . . Just for the heck of it though, I go to my parents' bathroom and get on the scales. Eighty pounds. How can Dad look like Cookie Monster and I'm skinnier than Elmo? Tall enough, but skinny. I push up my sleeve, check my muscles in the mirror. *Pathetic.*

"What are you doing?" Lizbreath is standing in the doorway staring at me. Good thing she can't read minds. Sesame Street? That's all I need.

"You are so strange," she says, adjusting her jeweled headband, stringing her black-painted fingernails through her purple-streaked long brown hair. She's trying to start a Cleopatra trend. So far she's the only taker. "Bring the garbage cans in before dinner, Kip. And sweep the sidewalk. Don't forget the sidewalk."

I skim my door and start math homework. Converting fractions into decimals. That gives me an idea. I head back downstairs, bike across town. It doesn't take long. Clover is small. If you blink when you sneeze, you could miss us.

Food? There's the Bumblebee Diner. Stew's mother, Mrs. Brumbaugh, runs it. Next corner up, Sal's Sips and Subs. Mobil station by the docks for candy.

Fun? Belcher's Bowling Alley. The Arcadia Theater, two screens. And Paulie's Pub has a pool table and dartboard in the back room, as long as we're out by six o'clock.

Friends? Tucker, Jupey, and Stew. We're all just a couple of blocks away.

I stop at Clover Stamp and Coin. I've never been inside before. I'm not the collecting kind. When I open the door, the guy at the counter jumps like I woke him up late for school. He wipes drool off his chin and stares at me.

"Say you had eighty pounds of gold," I say. "What would that be worth?"

The guy squints at me like I'm a worm. "What's it to you," he says.

"I have a school project . . . sir. Thanks."

"Okay," he says. The *sir* and *thanks* must have helped. He clicks on his computer. "Let's see." He gurgles up phlegm in his throat, hawks it into a handkerchief, looks at it, types something. "U.S.?" he asks.

"What?"

"You want to know U.S. conversion rates?"

"Sure."

"Well it's not as simple as that. There's U.S. . . . Euro . . . makes a difference."

"U.S., sir, thanks."

"Okay, let's see . . . exchange rate . . . gold . . . you said eighty pounds, right?"

"Yes."

"Right now gold's going off at five-ninety an ounce."

"Five dollars and ninety cents?"

"No." He laughs like I'm stupid. "Five hundred and ninety *dollars*."

Wow. That's a lot of money.

The guy clicks on a calculator. "Okay. How many ounces in a pound?"

"Sixteen," I say.

"Good. You're not as dumb as you look. So, sixteen times five hundred ninety dollars . . . let's see. . . that's nine thousand four hundred and forty dollars."

Oh my . . .

". . . times eighty is . . ."

Oh my . . .

"Roughly seven hundred and fifty-five thousand."

"Seven hundred and fifty-five thousand *dollars*?"

"No, doughnuts."

"Three-quarters of a million dollars?"

"Last time I counted."

"Holy ship!"

"Watch your mouth."

"Sorry." My heart is booming. "I said *ship*. Thank you, sir. Thanks a lot."

I speed back to the beach. The tide is in. The waves are crashing loud.

"Okay," I shout, all out of breath. "Okay. The gold. It's a deal."

Now the question is . . . do I tell my friends? Can I tell my friends?

But almost a million dollars?

A million dollars?

That changes everything.

CHAPTER 7

Tucker, Jupey, and Stew

That's the state to live and die in! . . . R – r – rich!
—Charles Dickens, *Our Mutual Friend*

I'm steam-shoveling scrambled eggs and pancakes with syrup into my mouth next morning when Dad sits down with the newspaper. I'm on my third helping, not wasting any time. Every pound, every ounce, is golden. I did the math last night.

All I have to do is help the dead get lighter, while I gain weight, nineteen pounds is all, up to 107 by next October, that's about a pound a month—how hard can that be?—and then I'm going to be rich. Richer than rich.

I'm going to be *a millionaire.*

"I don't understand," Dad says, shaking his head

over the obituary page. "We buried Jim Hennessey's whole family. His father, his grandmother, his aunt and uncle . . ."

Golden's Funeral Home beat us again. I picture their TV commercial. They look like a country club. Huge parking lot, waterfall by the entrance, four big, spacious viewing rooms, memorial music videos, "live broadcast of services to family and friends throughout the world"—all for less than we charge. What doesn't Dad understand? How can we compete with that?

"Didn't you ever hear of Q-tips?" Lizbreath's next to me. Her breath smells like Mosely's litter box. "Your ears are disgusting. You've got enough scum in there to grow—"

"Morning, Lizbeth," Mom interrupts. "Can I make you some eggs?"

"*No thank you.*" My sister is horrified. "Don't you people read the paper? All that cholesterol will kill you."

"Good," I say, "load her up." I smile at my mother. "See you later, Mom."

As I'm heading out, something wet hits me, like spit. I look back at Lizbreath.

"*Gotcha,*" Chick says, giggling, under the table. I can see the pink squirt gun.

"Fee . . . fi . . ." I shout, walking toward her with a monster face, arms in the air. Chick screams and tears off up the attic stairs, laughing. Nanbull and Aunt Aggie live up there. Chick can't run on our floor. No running, no noise, no nothing. But she can run crazy in the attic. Jump off the couch, dance, whatever.

It's Friday. "Guts" day. Guts is our clubhouse at Willow Grove Cemetery. You've got to have guts to belong. Tuck, Jupe, Stew, and me are the only members.

Tuck is waiting for me at the corner. "Hey dude," he says. "You do the math?"

"Yeah, sure." I hand him my notebook. We sit on old Mrs. Keating's steps, waiting for Jupey and Stew. Mrs. Keating doesn't mind, as long as we don't chuck gum on the ground or anything.

Tuck adjusts his glasses. A crummy blue Band-Aid holds the frame together from when he took a basketball in the face in gym. That was three months ago. Frames are expensive.

"I just need 18 and 24," Tuck says. "I got all the rest."

It's not that Tuck doesn't work hard, he does. School doesn't come easy though. "Learning disabilities," I've heard teachers say. They ought to whisper. Kids can hear.

Mr. Germano in third was the worst. What was that guy's problem, anyway? He stared at Tuck like Tuck was an idiot. "Are you with me, Tucker? Are you stuck again, Tucker? Stuck on directions? Stuck on a word? What are you stuck on, Tucker?" Pretty soon some kid said "stucker," and it locked like airplane glue. Forget ever peeling it off. Tuck's stuck with "Stucker" until we leave Clover and sail far away from here. To places where people don't know old nicknames or a family's business, either.

Tuck might be slow with school stuff, but he's fast when you need a friend. Stew and Jupey are my buddies too, but Tucker's my brother. Brown hair, blue eyes—we look alike. I'm skinnier, though. Tuck's dad hauls crab and lobster, and his mom sells them down at the docks. It's a tough way to make a living.

Stew and Jupey turn the corner. "Meatball subs for Guts," Stew shouts, holding up a sack. It's the size of a cooler you'd take to the beach. Stew's mom runs Bumblebee Diner, "Home of the Bee's-best Cooking in Clover." She keeps us stocked with good stuff.

Chili, brownies, pie. Meatball subs are my favorite. "How many you got?" I ask.

"Four," Stew says, tucking his shirt back over his belly, "but only one piece of apple pie." Rock-paper-scissors will settle that. Jupey always wins. He's the r-p-s champ. That and juggling. He won trophies for both at the Barnstable Fair.

"Did you hear the Coast Guard boats this morning?" Jupe says, turning his Yankee cap front to back. Jupe and Stew are Yankee fans. Tuck and I are Red Sox Nation.

"Helicopters been out since dawn," Jupe says. "Some dude's sleeping with the fishes for sure. My dad's down there now."

Jupey's father is a police officer, the first African-American sergeant in Clover. Jupe's real proud of him. They have matching buzz cuts and lift weights together. Jupe's parents are divorced. His mom moved to California. She tells people their future by reading star charts. Jupe sees her every other holiday and a month in the summer. He keeps hoping she'll come back, but I don't think that's in the stars.

We reach school just as Principal O'Brien is closing the front door.

"Gentlemen," she says, nodding at us. She tries to look mean, but she isn't.

"Guts at 4 o'clock," I call, and we scramble to beat the homeroom bell.

CHAPTER 8

"Guts"

*The whole difference between construction
and creation is exactly this: that a thing constructed
can only be loved after
it is constructed; but a thing created is loved before
it exists.*

—Charles Dickens

There's a new girl in homeroom. Our teacher, Mrs. Dermady, she's nice, says to "Please welcome Drew Callahan, our new harbormaster's daughter."

Drew Callahan is beautiful. I sneak peeks at her during the pledge. At lunchtime I discover, by the luck of alphabetical order, because Micky Connors moved to Texas, that Drew's locker is next to mine. Girls from our class stare and whisper as they pass, probably jealous because Drew's so beautiful.

Gigantic brown eyes, long chocolaty curls . . .

"Can I eat with you, Kip?" Drew says. She has an orange plastic flower sewn on her sweater; the petals almost look real.

"Sure," I say, feeling like I'm gonna puke. Puke in a good way, that is.

"So, your dad's the new harbormaster," is all I can think of to say.

"Yep," she says. "How about your dad? What does he do?"

Waves wash in over my brain and out again. "He's an entrepreneur," I say. "We're opening up a Super Seven Sports Center soon." *Liar.*

I used to be proud of Dad's job. When I was little, if we didn't have a call in, my friends and I played freeze-forever and hide-and-seek downstairs. No better hiding place than a coffin. But that was kindergarten. This is now. Now, Dad's job is freaky.

"Cool," Drew says. She means the Super Seven. "What sports do you play?"

Someone pushes my shoulder. "Hi, Flower Boy," Bub Jeffers says. He's with Dirk and two other Clover Clarions. They're wearing their green warm-up jackets with their names on them.

Bub smiles at Drew. He points to the flower.

"Gotta water that thing?" he says.

Drew laughs. "Just once a day," she says. She watches him walk down the hall.

I lead Drew to a table in the corner of the cafeteria, far away from Bub. We start to eat, no big deal. I've got ham and cheese. She's got peanut butter. "So, what sports do you play?" she says again.

A French fry lands on our table. I ignore it.

"Mostly baseball, now," I say. "How about you?"

"Basketball and track."

Another French fry lands on our table. Drew looks around to see who threw it.

"So, where did you live before here?" I ask.

Bub walks up to us. "Sorry about the fries," he says, smiling at Drew. "Bad aim." He picks one up and arcs it into a garbage can halfway across the room. Score.

"Nice shot," Drew says.

"So, Kip," Bub says, tossing another fry and making an easy basket. "How many dead bodies in your house this week?"

"*What?*" Drew says, looking at me, confused. "What's he talking about?"

The bell rings for next period. The lunch lady flicks the lights on and off.

"Didn't he tell you?" Bub says. "Kip lives in a funeral home."

"*Eeeeew,*" Drew says, scrunching up her face. Even scrunched, it's beautiful.

"Let's go, people," the lunch lady says, wiping off our table with a sponge.

"See you around, Drew. Later, Deadbo." Bub flaps his hands by his ears.

"You live in a funeral home?" Drew says as we walk to class.

"We inherited it," I say. "But we're moving as soon as we find the right location for the Super Seven."

"Oh, right," Drew says. "What's the 'seven' stand for?"

"Different sports. We're going to have indoor soccer, tennis courts, an Olympic size pool, a hockey rink . . ."

"Wow," Drew says. "That's awesome. Wait till I tell my dad."

After school, Drew asks me to show her around Clover. I'm late biking to Guts.

It was this time of year, right before Halloween, three years ago when we discovered it. Mr. Hewitt, our fourth-grade teacher, told us to search around town, looking for dates on old buildings and businesses. I knew where there was a really old number. *Willow Grove Cemetery, Est. 1879.* I'd passed it tons of times sitting next to Dad in Black Beauty. Dad's really proud of that hearse, polishes it before every funeral. "Our families deserve the best," he says.

Willow Grove is on a hill at the edge of town. Long ago, people used to stroll around and have picnics in cemeteries, like they were parks. Every May, Campbell's hosts "Remembering Day" here. Families bring flowers and stuff to decorate the grave sites and share stories about the people buried here. Then we have a big picnic. *60 Minutes* did a show about us once. Dad was proud.

So, anyway, Tuck, Jupe, Stew and I were looking for history at Willow Grove.

"Gold mine," Tuck said. "Look at these numbers. We're getting A's for sure."

Born 1892–Died 1914. Born 1899–Died 1950. Tons of history. Row after row.

We set off in different directions. It was quiet. The sun was setting.

"Hey guys," Stew shouted, "look at this." He was down in a far corner of the cemetery. I didn't remember us ever burying anybody back that far before.

It was a small wooden building, nearly hidden

behind the thick green reeds of an enormous willow tree. The biggest willow I'd ever seen.

My great-great-great-great-grandfather Christopher Adams Campbell planted the first willow tree here when the cemetery was founded, and all the Christophers have planted willows ever since. It's a Campbell and Sons tradition.

I brushed aside the jungle ropes so we could get a better view.

It was a barn, no, a shed maybe.

"Look," Tuck said, "the door is open."

Sure enough, it was. Cracked open an inch or so. A rusted padlock dangled down, unused. All of a sudden it felt colder.

"Who's going in?" Jupey said.

"Not me," Tuck said, stepping back like there was a fire.

"No way," Stew said. "There might be dead bodies in there."

"Yeah," Jupe said, "it's probably where they do the—" *Whoosh* . . . a gust of wind blasted by, rustling the willow reeds, slamming the door shut, scaring the bloody ghouls right out of us.

"Let's go," Stew said, shaking. "It's dinnertime anyway."

"Yeah, come on, guys," Tuck said. "I'm outta here."

Jupe stood there, staring at me. "I dare you, Kip."

"Dare me to what?"

"Go inside. See what's in there."

"Why me?" I said. "You do it."

"What's the matter, Kip," Jupe said. "You're not afraid of dead bodies, are you?"

I looked at the shed, at the spiderwebs dripping from the roof. The wind *whoosh*ed again. Stew jumped, all bug-eyed. "Come on, guys, now."

"I dare you, Kip," Jupey said again. "Go ahead. Go in. You're the funeral director's son. Don't you have the guts?"

That got me mad. "Yeah, I've got the guts. Guess I'm the only one."

Then I walked to that door, no looking back. It's like that first dive in May. The ocean's freezing. You've just got to do it. No toe testing. No baby steps. Just do it.

So I did. And that's the day we found Guts. We didn't build it, but it's ours. My whole life I wanted a tree fort, a big one, with a ladder and ropes to haul stuff. But you can't have a fort in your yard when you run a funeral home. Everything has to be neat, and mowed and trimmed and swept. Like nobody lives there.

Guts wasn't good at first. It was dark and damp and filled with junk. Old lawn mowers, weed trimmers, shovels and stakes, flower vases, cracked statues, grave markers, wreath wires. It smelled like dirt and gasoline and slimy grass clippings and something nasty we couldn't identify.

Later Nanbull told me the place was Johnny Abel's, the old caretaker's, shed. He was Willow Grove's outdoor guy. After he died, the town hired a landscaping company. I guess nobody cared about old Johnny's shed. We cared though. We cared a lot.

That's how we got Guts. And so far, it's our secret, just the four of us. One time Bub and Dirk saw us heading out of the gates. "What are you doing, Deadbo? Digging up bodies?" Jupey wanted to fight them, but I said no. Dad would be mad. Anyway, even if Bub and Jerk went looking, they wouldn't find Guts. The willow is great camouflage.

Everybody's at the table when I get to Guts. Stew's mom gave us the table and four chairs from the diner. We hauled them down on wagons attached to our bikes. The brown couch is new. Someone put it out on garbage day with a sign marked "Free." The price sounded good to us. Jupey's shuffling the cards. "Come on, Kip, let's go."

"Wait," I say. "What's in the icebox?" That's our antique refrigerator. Nanbull gave it to us. People kept food cold in there with ice before electricity was invented.

"Root beer," Tuck says. "I saved you one."

Stew opens the sack of meatball subs. "Still warm," he says, all happy.

I take a huge bite, smothered in mozzarella cheese. Almost as good as Sal Delicato's. I take another bite, thinking of the gold. Come on, calories, come to papa, *ca-ching, ca-ching*.

"Five card draw," Jupe calls, dealing. "Twos are wild."

I look at the stats board on the wall. The Sox are having a great season. The new pitcher was worth it. Yankees. Red Sox. We're divided down the middle. Two blue. Two red. We try to be civil, but if we both make it to the play-offs, there'll be trouble.

A ten, three jacks, and an ace. I throw in the ten, hoping for a full house or four of a kind. Tuck takes his time deliberating. I look at the blue trunk in the corner, covered with comics and swimsuit editions.

The day we found Guts, we hoped it was a treasure chest. We carried it outside, brushed off the cobwebs. I opened the latch. A black spider scurried out across my hand. I flung it away and shivered. Then we all dug in.

No treasures, nothing good, just some old men's clothes. We are disappointed. Tuck had to go. Jupe and Stew biked back to the diner for more stuff. I started looking through the clothes. Maybe there was money. I felt something hard, maybe a key, in a pocket.

No, a piece of jewelry. A clover, like the one on the town sign, except gold. It glinted in the sunlight. I stuck it in my pocket.

When I got home I threw it in my top drawer where I shove all my junk.

CHAPTER 9

Fish Food

He had but one eye,
and the popular prejudice runs in favor of two.

—Charles Dickens, *Nicholas Nickleby*

I wake up in a sweat, heart pounding, scared. The garage door is clanking open downstairs. I hear the motor humming, smell the exhaust fumes wafting up through the radiator. Dad is backing Black Beauty in with a body.

Nothing strange about it. Dad gets calls from the hospital or nursing home any time of the day or night. But there's something different about this one. I can feel it.

"Dad brought in Billy Blye last night," Mom says at breakfast, leaning in close as she pours my juice, so Chick won't hear. "Washed up on Newcomb Beach, bloated something awful. Been out there a while. They're still not sure how he died."

A freezing hand grips the back of my neck. "*Ahhh!*" I jump and reach to yank it away, knocking over my cereal bowl, spilling milk everywhere.

There's no hand, of course. Mosely purrs and closes his eyes again.

I picture Billy Blye's face, the sewn-up spot where an eye used to be.

"I'll help you Kip," Chick says, mopping up the milk with her napkin.

"Kip," Mom says, looking at me. "Are you okay?"

"Yeah, sure." My heart is racing. I lay my hands down flat on the table to stop them from shaking.

Mom's staring at me. "You're not still scared of that old blowhard, are you? No sense being . . ."

Billy Blye is in the basement. Billy Blye's in the freaking Frankenstein lab.

"Here, Kip," Chick says, sliding the cereal box toward me, giggling. She's got her cowgirl outfit on, wearing her sheriff's badge, pink water gun sticking out of her pocket.

"Thanks." I smile, but I'm not hungry anymore. I think I'm gonna puke.

Billy Blye. I remember that day my silver kite

landed on his roses. How he got so mad. Grabbed me by the back of my neck like I was a dog. I was so scared I nearly wet my . . . get a grip, Kip. You're twelve years old.

Billy Blye's dead. He's dead. Before I leave for school, I head down to the basement. I have to see for myself. My heart is drumming in my ears.

I'm no sissy cat around dead bodies. I've seen it all. Smashed-up faces, bashed-up skulls, brains and gook leaking out. I've watched Uncle Marty reconstruct noses and pump in the mothball juice, formaldehyde it's called, to preserve a body for viewing.

I don't ever want to do what Uncle Marty does, but I'm not afraid of it. Death is part of life. Nothing to be afraid of. We live, we die. That's how it is.

Billy Blye is another story.

The prep-room door is locked, that's the law, but I know where Dad keeps a key.

I flick on the light, smell that medicine smell.

It's cold in here. It has to be.

There's a white sheet drawn over Billy Blye's body.

I walk toward him, slowly.

The morgue ID tag is hanging from a toe. Some

fish had a feast with the others. Billy Blye, fish food.

I step forward, slowly, my heart hammering, *boom-boom-boom-boom-boom*. I want to see his face.

I start to sweat. Forget it. I turn to leave. I'm late for school.

And that's when I hear: *Hook knows the truth.*

I bolt out of there like a rocket ship, the silver door whooshing shut behind me.

CHAPTER 10

The Lucky One

Ever been the best of friends!

—Charles Dickens, *Great Expectations*

I bike to the beach after school, crawl out on my throne to think.

"No," I shout. "No way. No way am I helping Billy Blye."

The anchor's too heavy, Kip. He can't board.

Billy Blye's funeral is Friday. Dad is having trouble tracking down relatives. And Blye's body is in such bad shape, it will take Uncle Marty more time for restoration. He'll need extra Restowax for that body. One eye isn't all that's missing.

Restowax is like Silly Putty or modeling clay. Embalmers use it to shape body parts. Tuck and I used to make it into superheroes when we were little. Clover Cleptons, we called them. We tried selling the

Cleptons at the Christmas Bazaar. Aunt Aggie's friends thought they were "sweet" until we mentioned the Restowax; then they dropped the Cleptons like they were Mosely turds.

"How come Billy Blye gets to go to heaven? I thought you had to be good to get in? Blye was bad. Meaner than a rabid jellyfish. And not just to me. Every kid in Clover was afraid of him."

We have a deal.

"So what!" I think about the gold. "Can't you get someone else this time?"

You're the lucky one.

Yeah, right. I'm really lucky.

Then that's all. No more voices. Just wind. I climb back over the rocks to my bike. From here I can see the edge of Blye's property. Those stupid roses. "Come on," I shout. "Give me a break. There must be somebody . . ."

"Hey, Kip." Tuck is walking toward me. "Who are you talking to?"

"Nobody."

"I heard you, just now. You said…"

"Billy Blye's dead," I blurt out, trying to set Tuck's mind off track. "My father picked him up at the morgue last night."

"Yeah, Jupey told me," Tuck says, taking the bait. "His dad says it looks accidental, but they want to rule out murder. Murder. Imagine? Serves him right. Remember the time he cut the line on our raft 'cause we tied it on his dock? We were, what, seven? We didn't know it was his property. That was mean. Remember?"

"Yeah, I remember."

"And remember the Fourth of July he called the cops because we set off firecrack—"

"Tuck, I know, listen. I want to tell you something. Important. But you can't tell anybody."

Tuck looks at me. He nods.

"I know how we can make a lot of money."

"How much?"

"Three-quarters of a million dollars."

"*Whoa.*" Tuck turns and looks around behind us, lowers his voice. "Is it legal?"

I laugh. "Yeah, it's legal."

"What is it, the lottery? A gambling deal?"

"No. We have to find out what happened to Billy Blye."

"Billy Blye? *Whoa.* Why? Is there a reward for information? Jupe didn't say anything about a reward. His father would know if—"

"You've just gotta trust me, Tuck."

Tuck starts to say something, but stops. He nods his head. "Okay."

I clench my right fist, knuckles forward. Tuck does the same. One, two, three. Seal the deal. Got your back, dude.

"Where do we start?" Tuck says.

"First, we have to find some guy named Hook. He's got information."

"How do you know that?"

"I've got my sources." I think about Billy Blye's fish-food corpse down in the Frankenstein lab. Uncle Marty will be working on him all day long, classical music playing in the background. Dad will be on the phone trying to track down relatives to make the arrangements. Nanbull will write the obituary and send it over to the *Chronicle*. Aunt Sal will be wondering how to handle the matter of Blye's missing eye. Leave it be or cover it somehow? Mom will be contacting the clergy. All for Billy Blye.

Calling hours will be Thursday. The funeral, Friday morning. I don't have much time to find out what's keeping the old fish-turd from sailing.

When I get home, Mom says, "The lawn needs mowing, Kip."

I wheel out the John Deere and crank the engine. There's a paper on the lawn, in my way. I shut off the mower to pick it up. When I bend down, I see a clover.

I crouch closer. There's a bunch of them. One stands out, like it's calling to me. I snip its thin stem down by the roots and hold it up to look. Three dark green circles, then a fourth, smaller one. I stick it in my jacket pocket. It reminds me of the clover I found in the trunk at Guts. I've got to dig that thing out. Might be worth something.

After dinner I get on the scales. Eighty-two pounds. *Yes.*

CHAPTER 11

The Serious and the Smirk

She knows wot's wot, she does . . .

—Charles Dickens, *Pickwick Papers*

First thing next morning, I go upstairs to Nanbull's. My grandmother knows everybody in Clover. I'm hoping she knows "Hook."

Nanbull answers the door in a red velvet bathrobe. "Shhh," she says, holding her finger to her lips. "Aunt Aggie's not feeling well."

Nanbull quietly closes Aunt Aggie's bedroom door, snuffing out the awful snoring. Sounds like Stew practicing the tuba. "How can you sleep through that?" I say.

Nanbull rolls her eyes. "Funny thing, Ag doesn't even know she does it."

"You've never complained?"

"What good would it do? She's been snoring like that since she moved in after Gramp died. And you know Aggie. She's such a prissy goose, it would kill her if she knew she snored like a seal. Besides, she's getting old, and as long as I can hear her honking, I know she's still kicking." Nanbull winks at me and we laugh.

Nanbull makes me a mug of hot chocolate, plops in marshmallows. "Gotta fatten you up," she says. She sets two cinnamon rolls covered with frosting on a plate in front of me, then turns the knob on the range. She takes out butter, eggs, sausage, and bacon. "You're skinny as a pencil. What do they feed you down there? Raisins?"

I laugh. "Load me up, Nanbull. Every calorie counts." Nanbull looks at me funny, but doesn't ask what I mean.

When I was younger and Campbell's was busy, I use to come up here all the time for breakfast. Couldn't have the smell of bacon floating down to the funeral floor. When there's a call in, we know the rules. No cooking. No running. No nothing.

Up here in the attic, you can break the rules.

While Nanbull's cooking, I check out her living

room. Two blue chairs with matching footrests, tall brass lamps on the end tables. There's a wicker basket next to Aunt Aggie's chair, with jumbles of yarn and knitting needles inside. Mouse stuff.

There's a book on Nanbull's table, of course. She reads all the time.

David Copperfield.

I open the cover. Published in London in 1874. The pages are yellowed, sewn together at the binding. Must be really strong thread. The book smells old but good, sort of like dirt, sort of like Guts, but I'm not sure why.

Next to Nanbull's chair is her library case. Two rows of books all have the same black leather jackets, five bands of gold on the spines.

A Tale of Two Cities . . . *Oliver Twist* . . . The complete works of Charles Dickens. A present from Grandpa Campbell.

Nanbull's told me the story a million times. She saw the collection at an estate sale one summer, and it was "love at first sight." She knew they were too expensive and so she "didn't say a word." Grandpa saw her looking at them, but "he never let on."

Gramp went back later and placed a bid. Surprised her on Christmas morning.

"Better than diamonds or a mink coat or a trip around the world," Nanbull says, coming to stand beside me. "You can never be lonely with Dickens."

She takes *A Christmas Carol* off the shelf and fingers the title engraved in gold. "This is my favorite one, Kip," she says. "It always reminds me that as long as we're alive, no matter what we've done wrong, we still have a chance to make it right."

"I know the story, Nanbull. I saw the movie. The old miser, Ebenezer Scrooge, and the ghosts that come to teach him a lesson."

"That's right," Nanbull says, smiling. "And it's about a family pulling together and loving each other, even when times are tough."

Something about what Nanbull is saying makes me feel . . .

"Ta-da!" Nanbull flings her arms wide in front of the books like she's showing off the grand prize on a game show. "These will all be yours someday, Kip. I'm leaving them to you. Dickens deserves someone with a sense of humor. Someone who gets the 'serious and the smirk.' Heaven knows we need smirks in this business."

"Don't talk like that, Nanbull. You aren't going anywhere. Who would cook me bacon?" I nod toward the kitchen. "And make sure it doesn't burn."

"Oh dear gawd," she says, hurrying off, "we'll set off the smoke alarm."

I wolf down my food. Nanbull pours herself some tea and spoons more eggs on my plate. It's warm up here. When I take off my jacket, I remember the clover I found on the lawn. I take it out to show her.

"Aren't you the lucky one," Nanbull says, laying it on the table, and gently smoothing it out. "The Irish say the three leaves of the shamrock stand for the Trinity. Father, Son, and Spirit. Or for faith, hope, and love."

"And to remind us why we're here, right? To live, to love, and to leave something better behind."

"So you listen to me sometimes," Nanbull says.

"I listen to you a lot," I say. "But what does the fourth leaf stand for?"

Nanbull takes a sip of tea. "Some say it's the grace of God. It brings luck to the one who carries it. Four-leaf clovers are rare, you know."

"Here, you keep it, Nanbull."

"Oh no, dear boy, I'm as lucky as I can be. Give it to someone who needs it."

*

When I ask Nanbull about Billy Blye and some guy named Hook, she shakes her head, no. "Wait," she says. "Birdie O'Shaughnessy. She'll know."

"Who's Birdie O'Shaughnessy?"

"You know her, Kip. The lady who is always collecting stuff on the beach. She comes to all the wakes but never talks to anybody, makes Lizbeth so angry."

"The *Birdlady*? You're kidding."

"Don't call her that, Kip, it isn't nice. Bridget O'Shaughnessy, we called her Birdie for short. We went to high school together. She still lives over by the beach, I think. Tell her I sent you. She'll know me by my maiden name, Nora Fagan."

Nanbull knows the Birdlady?

"Birdie knows what's what on the shore side of Clover. She combs that beach every day. If anybody knows Blye's business, Birdie will. She used to be sweet on him when we were young, before Billy got married."

CHAPTER 12

The Birdlady

A wonderful fact to reflect upon,
that every human creature is constituted to be
that profound secret and mystery to every other.

—Charles Dickens, *A Tale of Two Cities*

Who knew the Birdlady had a name? Bridget O'Shaughnessy. *Birdie.*

Nanbull said Birdie was normal way back in high school, had friends and everything. But after they graduated, something happened. Birdie stopped talking to people. "Holed herself away like a hermit crab," Nanbull said. Nobody knew why.

Tuck and I see her on the beach all the time. Walking along, picking up junk, tossing food to birds. Sometimes even has a gull perched on her shoulder. Dad says she's a woodle. I say she's crazy.

Crazy or not, after school, I bike to the beach to find the Birdlady.

Tuck couldn't come. He had to stay for extra help. I'm not getting Stew and Jupe involved yet. Jupey will want to lead the investigation, and Stew talks too much.

As soon as I reach the beach, I spot her. She's walking with her yellow PriceCheck bags, wearing a raincoat and hat even though it's not raining, her gray hair straggling down like dried seaweed.

She stops to inspect something. Picks it up. Puts it in a bag, moves on.

I walk down the steps and come up behind her slowly so I won't scare her. "Excuse me, Miss O'Shaughnessy."

She snaps around, eyes wide as full moons. "Not me," she says, and takes off.

I follow. "My grandmother sent me. You're Bridget O'Shaughnessy, right?"

She hurries faster, the yellow PriceCheck bags bumping against her legs. The bag on the right is full of cans. For the deposits, probably. The one on the left is filled too. A red plastic shovel and a magazine stick out the top.

"Please, wait. I just want to ask you a question. About Billy Blye."

The Birdlady stops. She sets down her bags.

I walk around to face her, but she won't look at me. She shakes her head, turns away. "Poor Billy," she says in a gruff voice, but sad, like she misses him.

"Miss O'Shaughnessy, I need your help. My grandmother said that—"

"Who's that?"

"Nora Fagan," I say.

Birdie's wrinkled face is blank, but then she nods, wipes her nose with the back of her hand. Her nails are dirty. She fumbles in her pocket, takes out a stubby cigarette. She has a hard time with the wind, but finally lights a match, takes a puff, then hands it to me like she's sharing.

"No, thanks." I step back, disgusted. "I don't smoke."

"Nora Fagan's a good girl," Birdie says, taking a deep drag of the cigarette. "We was friends once." She slowly blows out the smoke. "Long ago." She stands fixed like a statue at St. Mary's. Not moving, not talking, just staring out at the waves like she's in another world, someplace I'm not.

I check my watch. I'm late for dinner. No calling hours tonight, so it might be a decent meal that involves cooking. "Were you and Billy Blye friends?" I ask.

Birdie doesn't answer me.

"I mean, did you know him?"

"'Course I knew him." She laughs. Her teeth are yellow. "Lived up there." She motions to the gray cottage on the bluff. "Saw him near every day. Heard him cryin', too."

"Crying?" I say, finding it hard to picture that. "Why was he cry—?"

"That's Billy's business," she shouts. She comes closer, the burning tip of the cigarette nearly touching my face. "Don't go nosin' in other people's business. Ya hear me? People's entitled to their secrets. Ya hear me? Now get outta here."

She picks up her bags and walks.

"Wait, Miss O'Shaughnessy, please. I'm not trying to be nosy, really. Billy himself asked me to . . ."

She turns back, walks up close, sticks her face right near mine. She smells like tuna. Her storm-blue eyes study mine. "Billy's dead," she says, and turns away.

Just go for it, tell her the truth. Who's she going to tell, anyway? Even if she said anything, everybody thinks she's crazy.

"I know he's dead. But sometimes the dead have to lighten a burden before they can sail. And sometimes I help . . ."

"Stop," Birdie says, thrusting her palm toward my mouth as if to silence me. Her eyes shimmer like stars on her sun-darkened face. "So yer the lucky one now, are ya?"

Goose bumps pop out on my arms. "What do you mean, the 'lucky one'?"

"The clover," Birdie says. "The gold one. So yer the one got it now?"

My heart is pounding. "How do you know . . ."

"Never mind," Birdie says. She looks up and down the beach as if to check if anyone's coming. "I'll help you, just this once. But don't come back, ya hear me?"

"Okay," I say, "I won't. I promise. Just tell me who . . ." I lower my voice to a whisper. "Just tell me who Hook is and where I can find him." My body is shaking.

"*Hook!*" Birdie bursts out, laughing. "*Hook!*" She throws back her head, cackling. I see black holes where teeth used to be. It's not a pretty sight.

"Is that all ya want to know?" she says, wiping her eyes. "*Hook?*"

"Yes." She's a woodle all right. "Who is Hook?"

"Mother Mary," she laughs, holding her stomach, "saints preserve us, that's a good one."

An orange speckled butterfly flits past us. Then another.

"Monarchs," the Birdlady says to no one in particular, "sailing off to Mexico."

She stands there staring after them. She has a sad look on her face.

"Excuse me," I say, "but can—"

"C'mere," Birdie says, snapping out of it. She looks all around the beach again, then beckons me to come closer.

I hesitate.

"Whattarya, *scared*?" she says. "C'mere. I gotta whisper it."

I move toward her. She cups her hand around my ear. I try not to flinch.

"Hook's a bird," she says.

"*What*?" I back away. She's a woodle all right. "A *bird*?"

"Hook is Billy's parrot," she says. "*Ooooooh, scary. Oooooh, scary.*" Birdie flickers her fingers in the air by her eyes to look spooky.

She succeeds.

"Hook'll be in Billy's kitchen if you dare. *Ooooohh, scary,*" she says. She walks away, laughing, cans jangling against her leg.

Another monarch flits past me, so close I can see the pattern on its wings. When it passes by the Birdlady, she waves at it. "Have fun in Mexico!" she shouts.

CHAPTER 13

Hook

There's light enough for wot I've got to do . . .

—Charles Dickens, *Oliver Twist*

It's still dark when I wake Wednesday morning. I open the window in the kitchen to check for rain, and before I can stop him, Mosely pops the screen and leaps over to Uncle Marty and Aunt Sal's house. He's going to visit his cousins, Winken, Blinken, and Nod. Uncle Marty will bring him back when he comes to work.

I don't know how Mosely leaps that far. It's like he's Supercat or something. I'm going to buy him a cape for Christmas.

I write Mom a note that I've got early band practice, grab a flashlight, sneak down the stairs, and bike to the beach. It's cool and the fog is thick.

There's yellow police tape all around Billy Blye's

property. No cars though. Good. The pink roses that covered his fence all summer are dried-up now; the seedpods look like cherry tomatoes, the leaves and thorns, brown. These roses grow wild along the beaches here, ordinary as dandelions, but Blye acted like they were golden. He used to sit guard on his porch in the summer, making sure nobody touched his roses.

He chased me and Tucker off with a broom when we were, like, three or four and tried picking some for our mothers. And then there was the kite day. I shiver, remembering how I pricked my fingers bloody and how Blye scared the ghouls out of me. "I'll trap ya like a lobsta and boil ya till ya scream!" I ran home crying but went back the next day, braver. He had no right. That was my kite. I almost got the courage to knock on the door, but I turned sissy-cat chicken guts and ran.

But Billy Blye is dead now and pretty soon he'll be gone for good.

I slip under the yellow tape and unlatch the gate. It creaks as I push it in. The grass is knee-high. I stumble over something. I flick on my flashlight. A rusted fishing pole, jutting out like a trap.

I move the light around the yard. Lobster cages

scattered everywhere, covered with dried seaweed and moss. Back in the corner, a fishing boat, covered with tarp.

Funny, I never saw Blye out on the water. Tuck's dad's a fisherman. I know most of the guys. Never saw Billy on the beach, either, hardly ever in town. I think about the Birdlady saying she heard him crying. What was that about? Strange.

The steps squeak as I walk up to Blye's door. Get a grip, Kip. He's dead.

I try the handle. Locked.

Around the side of the cottage, there's a window, too high off the ground. I drag over a lobster cage and then another, make myself a ladder and climb. I wipe the dirt off the pane and look in.

A kitchen. So far so good.

I set down the flashlight, push against the window with both hands. It moves inward. *Squawk! Squawk!* The sound startles me and I fall backward, hitting my head on the ground, hard. That must be Hook still screeching inside. My heart is pounding.

It's a bird, Kip, a bird.

I restack the cages, climb back up, push the pane in all the way. I hoist myself up and dive in, remembering I forgot to pick up the flashlight.

I land in a sink. It's dark, I can't see. I hear a shuffling sound in the corner. My heart beats faster. I feel for the counter and crawl slowly, carefully, along it until I reach the end. I put up my palm, find the wall, search along it for a light switch. Got it.

"*Akillder, akillder,*" Hook squawks. I gulp and try to calm down.

The bird is in a silver cage in the corner. He's got a blue-and-green head and rainbow feathers. Some sort of tropical parrot. Hook looks at me, takes a sip of water, and flits onto a trapeze thing. He swings back and forth, "*Akillder, akillder.*"

What's 'akillder'?

I look around the room. Pretty normal. Refrigerator, stove, table with two chairs. A yellow storm slicker hanging on a hook by the door. A clock ticking. A calendar on the wall. I go to take a closer look. Black *x*'s marked over each date. A circle around October 12. That was three days ago. Maybe the day Billy drowned. I shiver. Strange.

"Kip!" someone shouts, and my heart nearly freezes. I turn to the window.

Tuck's goofy face looking in at me. "What are you doing," he says.

"What are *you* doing," I say, relieved.

"Following you. I saw you bike past. I was helping Dad stock bait. I thought we were in this together, Kip. You said . . ."

"Sorry, Tuck. I'm glad you're here. Come on in. I want to see if Blye's bird knows what happened to him. It's a parrot. He talks."

"Cool." Tuck slides down into the sink, hops down on to the floor. We approach Hook's cage together.

I stick my finger in. "Hey, Hook, hey, buddy."

The bird flies about, all crazy. *"Akillder, akillder, squawk, squawk."*

"He's scared," Tuck says.

"I know." I try talking in a gentler voice. "You must miss Billy, huh, buddy? You must be wondering who's going to take care of you now, huh, boy?"

"You're talking to him like he's a cat or a dog," Tuck says. "It's a *bird*."

"Well then you try," I say. "I don't know how to talk to birds."

Tuck unlatches the cage. "Maybe if we let him out, he'll lead us to a clue. Maybe he knows where the million dollars is stashed." Tuck pulls something out of his pocket. "A granola bar, strawberry." He breaks off a piece, offers it to Hook flat out on his palm.

Hook cowers back in a corner.

"Probably likes blueberry better," I say. "It's okay, Hook." I try again, sticking my hand in to pet a feather. "I just need you to help us. Then maybe we can help you find a new owner. Billy told me you could—"

"Billyboy akillder."

"What did you say?" Tuck is looking at me, spooked. "What do you mean, Billy told you something. Billy's dead. How could Billy . . ."

"Billyboy, billyboy, akillder, akillder," Hook screeches, louder now.

Then for a second, Hook's beady eyes meet mine. *"I killed her. I killed her."*

This time, my Dumbos hear him loud and clear. My body's an ice cube. The bird is repeating something he heard. He must have heard Billy say, "I killed her."

"Who did Billy kill, Hook?"

The bird backs away.

"Whoa, Kip," Tuck says, "you're freaking me out, dude. What do you mean, Billy killed somebody?"

"Come on, Hook," I get closer to the bird. I stare in his eyes. "Who did Billy kill? *Who*?"

There's a car outside. Doors slamming. Men's

voices. Tuck and I look at each other. We move fast toward the window, but we're too late.

There's a key in the lock, the door opens. "Freeze!"

Tuck and I turn around, hands in the air like in the movies. My body's shaking, my legs are pizza dough. Jupey's father, Sergeant Johnson, is pointing a gun at us.

"Fergimmecarry," Hook screeches all crazy in his cage. *"Fergimmecarry, squawk, squawk, fergimmecarry, please."*

CHAPTER 14

Liar Land

"Dombey and Son" . . .
Those three words conveyed the one idea
of Mr. Dombey's life . . .
He had risen, as his father had before him . . .
from Son to Dombey . . .

—Charles Dickens, *Dombey and Son*

"You've got some serious explaining to do, son," Dad says to me.

We are standing in the foyer of Campbell and Sons, the long line of Christophers staring down on me. I stare back at them. So what, mind your own business, you're dead.

Jupe's father drove me and Tuck here in the squad car. Siren off, good thing.

My father is looking at me with such disappointment, I'm afraid I'm going to bawl. Letting my dad down is the worst punch-in-the-gut feeling in the world.

I clench my fists to be strong, look past my father to the parlor, where Billy Blye's wake will be. It's all his fault. I can't believe I was trying to help . . .

"And you're certain Jupiter wasn't involved in this?" Sergeant Johnson asks.

Jupiter is Jupe's real name. His mother wanted something "original." Then she left Jupiter and his dad and took off to LA to tell horoscopes. That was original.

"No sir," I say. "Jupe didn't know anything about this. He's at school, I'm sure."

"I'll leave you to handle this, Boss," Sergeant Johnson says, putting his police cap back on. He adjusts it in the mirror, nods at me like he means it.

"Thank you, Sergeant," Dad says. He opens the door, pats Jupe's dad on the back. He lowers his voice. "Thank you, Miles. I appreciate your discretion on this."

"No problem, Chris. They're good kids," Sergeant Johnson mumbles. Then, in a louder voice, "Come on, Tucker. Let's get you home."

"Call me," Tuck says as he heads out the door, face pale as a shark's belly.

Tuck's scared. His dad is mean when he's mad. Hopefully Mr. Tobin had a good haul today. The fishermen have been complaining. It's been a bad October.

"Let's talk in here," Dad says, leading me into the parlor.

It smells like flowers and furniture polish. There's a box of tissues on the table, a dish of red-and-white peppermints. The toilet flushes upstairs.

"What were you thinking of, son? Trespassing on private property. Violating a police barricade . . ."

"I'm sorry, Dad." I cut him off before the list gets longer.

"Sorry? That's not enough, Kip. Why would you do such a thing?"

The word *gold* pops up in my mind like a Ping-Pong ball on the lottery show. I push it back down.

"I'm waiting, son." Dad is staring at me, his big brown eyes sad and confused like a honey bear in a movie.

"My kite," I blurt out, feeling a punch in my gut.

Fibbing about band practice is one thing. Lying straight to Dad's face is another.

"*What?*" Dad says.

I stare at the peppermints. "Billy Blye took the kite you gave me . . ."

Dad touches my arm. "Look at me, Kip." He's not buying this. "That was years ago. You haven't even mentioned that kite since—"

"But I never forgot, Dad," I say loudly. I stand up, move toward the doorway. I see the Christophers and turn back around.

Now that I'm smack in Liar Land, I'm starting to get my sea legs. I make a mad look on my face. "He had no right, Dad," I shout, getting myself worked up good. "Billy Blye had no right to keep that kite. You ordered it special from that catalog for my birthday, remember?" My face is red, body shaking. I bite my lip like I'm trying not to cry.

"It's okay," Dad says. He wraps his arm around me. "I understand. I didn't realize it was so important to you. I just wish you had told me."

Now I really feel awful. *Liar.* Now I really do start to cry.

Through the doorway I lock eyes with a Christopher, staring out of his golden frame, so serious and important. A Campbell father. A Campbell son. A pillar of the Clover community. He probably never lied. *Liar.*

For a second, I think about telling Dad the truth. About the voices and the anchors and the ship and the gold.

"Let's put this behind us for now, son. Come on, I'll drive you to school."

In the car Dad says, "I met the new harbormaster at the Lodge last night. Callahan is his name. Says his daughter's in your class. He wanted to hear more about the Super Seven Sports Center."

I steal a quick side look at my dad. His face is more sad than mad. The best father a kid could ever have, and I hurt him worse than the cowboys.

I get out of the car fast so he won't see me bawling.

Later, in math class, I start thinking about this morning. Hook saying Billy killed somebody. But who? And what does "fergimmecarry" mean?

I write "fergimmecarry" in my science notebook. I look at it for a long time. Nothing.

I try breaking it up into parts. Like "akillder" was really "I killed her."

I write: "Fer. Gim. Me. Carry."

I stare at the words in social studies. Finally in English, it hits me.

Forgive me, Kerry. That's what Hook was saying. Forgive me, Kerry.

Now who is Kerry? And why did Billy kill her?

CHAPTER 15

Birdie O'Shaughnessy's Cottage

*The place . . . was one of those receptacles for old and
curious things which seem to crouch in odd corners
of this town, and to hide their musty treasures from
the public eye . . .*

—Charles Dickens, *The Old Curiosity Shop*

After school at our lockers I see Tuck's face as he packs
up. His dad was out on the boat when Jupe's father
brought him home in the squad car this morning.
But Mr. Tobin will be there now. Tuck's mother will
have told him what happened at Billy Blye's cottage.
Mr. Tobin isn't a big talker, not a big listener, either.
He hits first, listens later. And if his nets were empty

again and he's already drinking, it could be real bad for Tuck tonight.

"I'll go home with you," I say. "I'll tell him it was my idea."

"No," Tuck says. "That'll make him more angry. He'll say 'Whaterya, a sissy, bringing home Kip to take the heat for you.'"

"Stay close to your mom tonight, Tuck."

"Yeah, whatever. Don't worry about me."

"Hey, Tuck, wait." I dig in my pocket for the four-leaf clover I found on the lawn. It's limpy and crumpled. I hand it to Tuck.

Bub Jeffers and Dirk Hogan are watching us.

"What's the matter with you, Stuck-*er*," Bub says. "You look like you're gonna bawl. Whatja lose your teddy bear?"

"Shut up, Blubber," I say.

Bub looks like he got stung by a jellyfish. "You talking to me, Deadbo?"

Dirk-the-jerk is speechless. Nobody talks to Bub Jeffers that way.

"Move along, boys." Principal O'Brien is walking toward us with a clipboard. "Don't you have somewhere to be, Mr. Jeffers?" she says to Bub. She nods in the direction of her office. Bub probably got detention again.

"Have fun, *Blubber*," I say real low as he passes by.

"You're dead, Dead—"

"Move along, Mr. Jeffers," Principal O'Brien says again. "You, too, Mr. Hogan."

It takes Dirk a second, probably wondering where "Mr. Hogan" is, then he gets it and gives the principal a nasty look. He's just smart enough to keep his mouth shut though. "Hope you find your *teddy bear*," he says to Tuck as he leaves.

Tuck's face is lobster red. I hate them for picking on him. They won't let Tuck forget that stupid bear his mother packed for a Cub Scout campout. Tuck didn't know the bear was there. Sometimes mothers don't have a clue just how badly they can screw things up.

"Good luck, buddy," I say to Tuck. "Call me if you need me."

I rush to my bike. Time is running out. Billy Blye's wake is tomorrow, the funeral, Friday. I've got to find out who he killed. That must be the anchor that's weighing him down. He murdered somebody. That would do it. Maybe the Birdlady can help again.

The Birdlady is my only hope.

It's raining. I bike toward the beach, tipping my Sox cap down. I never wear a jacket until it snows. Tuck, Jupe, Stew, none of us do.

Billy Blye's obituary was in the *Clover Chronicle* this morning. Nanbull did a good job finding nice things to say about the old fish-turd. Billy was married. His wife's name was Annie. She "predeceased" him, drowned at sea in a storm. They didn't have any children. Billy used to be the top lobsterman in Clover. "Cap'n Billy" trapped a sixty-pounder, the largest recorded around here. After everybody took pictures, Billy threw the big clawer back in. That was nice of him.

Mrs. Blye always won the blue ribbon at the Cape Cod Chowda Festival. The judges said there was a certain "sweet ingredient" they couldn't identify. Restaurants offered her big money for the recipe, but Annie Blye wouldn't divulge her secret.

Dad finally located a next of kin. A niece from Vermont, writes romance novels. She hasn't seen her uncle in years, but she's making the trip to Clover for the services, "because it's the right thing to do." She'll probably be the only one there. Well, no. Father Tallman, Doc Burton, the Birdlady, and her.

I think about Hook, wonder how he's doing. Jupe said his father took Hook over to Wayshak's pet store. They're waiting to see if a relative comes forward to claim him. I'm thinking if Billy Blye's niece doesn't want him, I know somebody who'd take good care of a bird.

I leave my bike at the top of the bluff. The wind is stronger now, rain pelting on me. It's getting dark and it's not even dinnertime. Must be near daylight savings. Turning the clocks soon. Won't be many more nights at Guts. We don't have electricity.

I look up and down the beach. No Birdlady. No anybody. No one on the water, either. Just the lighthouse on Cleveland Ledge, blinking steady through the mist.

The Birdlady must live near the water, carrying all those bags on the beach. She said she heard Billy Blye crying, so she must live near him. I head to Billy's cottage.

The police tape is gone. The place looks deserted. Dad said they concluded the investigation. Cause of death was "accidental drowning."

I walk around back. There's a shed and a big boat covered in tarp and behind it a thick wooded area.

It's hard to see with the rain, but *yes* . . . there's a pathway.

The brush is thick. I push wet branches away from my face. A pine bough snaps back, just missing my eye. Off to the right, there's a clearing.

A small tan cottage, no bigger than a shack, smoke swirling from the chimney.

The Birdlady's house. It must be. I look around the yard. There are bird things everywhere. Birdhouses, bird feeders, birdbaths. No birds, of course. It's raining. Birds are smart enough to take cover.

I'm soaked and my teeth are chattering. There's a nice warm smell coming from the house. Soup or stew.

By the door I think I hear someone talking inside, but when I knock, it stops.

"Who's there?" I recognize Birdie's voice.

"It's Kip, Miss O'Shaughnessy. Nora Fagan's grandson. We met on the beach."

"Not home."

"Please, Miss O'Shaughnessy. It will only take a minute."

"Get away before I call the p'lice."

"Oh, don't do that." That's all I need. Jupey's dad showing up again.

"Private property. Go away."

"Can I please just come in for a minute? It's pouring out here and I'm cold."

There's a long silence. Then a latch clicks open, then another, and another. She's got the place locked up like a bank vault.

The door opens an inch or so. An eye peers out at me.

"All right," she says, "ca' min. But jus' till ya dry off."

"Thank you." I enter, dripping wet.

She backs away, nervous. Why would she be scared of me?

Birdie rubs her hands together like she's washing them. "Over there." She motions to the chair by the fireplace. "I'll get ya a towel."

I sit, and lean in toward the flames, holding my hands close for warmth. It's dark in here. Except for the fire, the only light is the one from the burner on the kitchen stove.

There's a table right beside me, covered with things. I look closer. Strips of paper, magazines, scissors . . . a memorial card from Abe Banfield's wake.

A shadow flits across the wood floor in front of

the hearth, and for a second I think it's a bird. Maybe this is where all the birds are tonight. Maybe she's got them living right in here with her . . . *Hsssssssssss* . . . The pot on the stove is bubbling over. "Miss O'Shaughnessy, something's burning!"

She hurries toward me with two towels, then rushes out to the kitchen. She turns down the flame, lifts the lid, stirs whatever's inside.

"Smells good," I say, trying to be nice.

"I'm not invitin' ya ta dinner."

"No, I didn't mean that." I dry off my face, blot my shirt to soak up the water.

"What's yer name agin?" Birdie steals a quick look at me.

"Kip. You know my grandmother, Nora. Nora Fagan."

Birdie nods. "Nora's a nice girl," she says, sounding more relaxed.

I don't have much time. Mom and Dad will be wondering where I am. After what happened this morning, I can't afford to be late for dinner. I stand up. "Miss O'Shaughnessy . . ."

"Call me Birdie." She stirs the pot again.

Good. "Okay, Birdie." I walk toward the kitchen.

"I found Hook like you told me. Thank you. But he said something I couldn't understand and . . ."

"And ya think I know bird talk," she says, laughing. "I'm no bird."

Good. Laughing is good. "I know," I say. "But I thought maybe you might know someone named Kerry."

"That's who Billy picked." She shakes salt and pepper into the pot.

"Picked for what?"

"For his bride," Birdie says in a quieter voice, but my satellites hear her clearly.

I turn back toward the fireplace. "His bride?"

"His bride, his wife. Kerry was Billy's wife."

I'm confused. "But Billy's wife's name was Annie. I read it in the obituary in the paper this morning."

"That's right," Birdie nods. She slurps a taste of her dinner, shakes in more salt. "But Billie called her *Kerry* 'cause her people were from County Kerry. Ireland."

Forgive me, Kerry. Forgive me, Kerry. That's what Hook said. Hook must have heard Billy saying that.

"Oh my God. Billy killed his wife!"

"*Billy did not.*" The Birdlady rushes toward me with a dripping spoon in her hand. "Ya little liar.

Billy didn't kill nobody. Get outta here." Her eyes are flickering wildly.

I back away. "But that's what Hook said. He said, 'Billy killed her. Forgive me, Kerry.'"

"Oh . . ." The Birdlady sinks into the chair. The only chair. "Poor Billy," she says sadly. "Poor Billy." She looks into the fire, shaking her head.

"Ya gotta go, Billy," she whispers, but my Dumbos hear. "Kerry's waiting fer ya, dear boy, just go."

"Miss O . . . Birdie," I say in a gentle voice. "Then how did Kerry die?"

"*Twas an accident*," Birdie screams. She stares moon-eyed into the flames.

I don't say anything. I just stand there waiting, hoping she'll say something more.

Another shadow moves across the wood floor.

I look up, spooked, raising my arm to protect my eyes, certain there are birds flying around loose in here. And that's when I see them.

The paper cranes.

Hundreds of them.

All different colors and sizes.

Beautiful graceful paper birds swinging on strings from the rafters.

CHAPTER 16

The Secret

The seamen said it blew great guns.

—Charles Dickens, *David Copperfield*

"It was ten years ago this month, their anniversary, October 12," Birdie says. "I know the date 'cause I was in their wedding. Only one I was ever in. Wore a yellow dress, I did."

Birdie stares at the fire as she talks.

It's like she doesn't know I'm here.

"There was a nasty storm brewin', a nor'easter, and they ordered all boats off the water. But Billy was pulling good that year and wanted to haul in his cages. Kerry begged him not to go, but Billy was a stubborn goat.

"Kerry said she'd go with him. Billy said no. Kerry stood strong. She could be a goat too. Finally, Billy gave in. They headed out to where the traps were set.

Billy threw the anchor and they went to work. Soon, the sky turned black as coal and the clouds cracked open like eggs. Rain fell so hard ya couldn't see an arm's length in front a ya. But they kept workin', side by side. The waves got higher and higher, the boat was taking water, but they kept at it till the whole catch was in.

"Kerry was kneeling on the deck latching the ice lockers, and Billy was hauling up the anchor, when a beast of a wave knocked Billy back and the anchor crashed down on Kerry's head. Then a devil wave flipped the boat over and swept them into the sea."

Tears are rolling down Birdie's wrinkled face. Her arms are crossed tight over her chest, and she's rocking back and forth. I feel sorry for her. She wipes her nose with the back of her hand. I wish I had a tissue to give her.

"Billy searched and searched all night fer Kerry. Screamin' her name, tryin' to spot her in the dark, the waves high as houses. He swam frantic to keep his head above water. Lookin' for her. Lookin' for her. Nearly drowned himself. A nasty jagged thing caught Billy in the eye, but he kept searching, screaming for Kerry."

Now it makes sense why Billy cried at night. He was probably remembering . . .

"A boat out of Bramble found Billy around midnight and brought him in to shore. Billy collapsed near dead on the beach, wailing like a banshee, '*Kerry . . . Kerry . . .*'

"I brought blankets and a thermos, tried to get him to the hospital. 'Save yer eye, Billy.' But, no, he wouldn't move. Next mornin' Kerry's body came in with the tide."

We both stare at the fire. It hisses and a spark spits out by my sneaker.

"All this time," Birdie says, "Billy kept it a secret. Couldn't bare for Clover to know he was the one killed Kerry."

"But he didn't kill her," I say loudly. "It was an accident."

"That's right," Birdie says, leaning forward, looking at me like she just saw me for the first time. "That's right, Kipper. That's what I said. The undertaker did too."

"The undertaker?" I get a queasy feeling. *Undertaker* is the old-fashioned name for funeral director.

"That's right. Up at Campbell and Sons. The big, tall man, nice man. He saw Kerry's skull, and asked Billy about it. Billy told him. The undertaker said it wasn't the anchor killed Kerry; it was the storm. It was a miracle either one of them survived those waves. The undertaker said it was an accident. That was all people needed to know. He fixed up Kerry's face real nice for the wake. Everybody said she looked beautiful."

CHAPTER 17

The Truth

It was true…as turnips is.
It was as true…as taxes is.
And nothing's truer than them.

—Charles Dickens, *David Copperfield*

Leaving Birdie's, I bike home along the water. The rain
has stopped. I hear waves lapping against the docks,
buoys clanking, a horn from a boat that braved the
rain. Thick sheets of fish-smelling fog roll over me. I
think about Billy Blye.

It was an accident, Billy. You didn't kill Kerry. You
didn't do anything wrong. Except for being a royal
fish-turd to me about your stupid rosebushes . . .

Tell me truth, Kip.

What truth?

What happened the night of the storm.

The streets are empty. It's dark now. The Bumblebee

casts the brightest light. Just one customer at the counter. Mrs. Bee smiles as she pours him coffee. Stew's probably in the kitchen doing dishes. It's just the two of them. Stew's dad is gone.

I think about Tuck. How scared he was to go home. I hope his dad wasn't too hard on him.

Tell me truth, Kip.

Kerry's death was an accident, Billy. What's the big deal?

Tell them I killed her.

But Nanbull already wrote your obituary. It was in the paper this morning.

Write a new one.

I can't. Besides, nobody's blaming you for anything. You didn't mean to . . .

It's my anchor, Kip. Please.

Turning in to our driveway, I think about my dad. "The undertaker," Birdie called him. How he kept it secret about the anchor hitting Kerry Blye's head in that storm. Probably used Restowax to seal her skull. Dad did all the embalming before Uncle Marty joined the business. What other secrets is Dad holding inside? I wish I could talk to him.

Will he be mad if I write the truth about that accident ten years ago? *Whoa*, wait a minute, what if he could get in trouble for not reporting her head wound? What if he broke some code, some law? What if helping Billy Blye will hurt my father? I am so confused.

When I get home, I run up to the attic to tell Nanbull to write a new obituary for Billy Blye.

"But I already wrote . . ."

"Nanbull, it's *important*."

She studies my face. "Is this like when we drove to Boston to see Abe Banfield's son?"

"Yep."

"Okay, then." She goes to her desk. When she turns on the light, I see her smiling to herself, like maybe she understands more than she's letting on.

"Writing gets better with revision anyway," she says.

As I tell Nanbull about the night Kerry Blye died, something keeps gnawing on my brain. I understand, now, why Billy was so mean. He was carrying around an awful secret. But why was he so crazy about those roses?

"Hold it, Nanbull," I say as she's typing. "I might have one more thing to add."

"Make it a colorful detail, Kip," she says as I head out the door. "But hurry or we'll miss the deadline for the morning paper."

"How much time do I have?"

Nanbull looks at her watch. "Half hour, tops. And then we've got the wake . . ."

When I bolt down the stairs, Mom calls to me. "Kip, wait. Mosely's been missing all day. Keep your eye out for him."

"It's okay, Mom. He's probably visiting his cousins."

I bike to Wayshak's pet store. I'm hoping Hook can help me.

The store is closed, but I see a worker cleaning out the cages and knock.

"I need to talk to the bird," I say. "Hook."

"Is that his name?" the lady says, letting me in. "Sure, go right ahead. That poor parrot blabs all day long. He's sure missing somebody."

"Hi, Hook," I say, putting a finger in the cage. "Hi, buddy."

Hook tilts his head toward me, then away, but doesn't say anything.

"I know it's lonely in here, Hook. You'll have a new home, soon, I promise. I don't have much time now. I need your help. I need to know about the roses."

"Kerry's roses, blue ribbons, hmmm, hmmm, good."

Blue ribbons. Nanbull said Mrs. Blye always won blue ribbons for her chowder.

"Thanks, Hook. I'll be back for you soon. I promise."

I pedal fast to Billy's house, drag over the lobster cages, climb up and through the window. In the kitchen, I open up cabinets and drawers. Find some cookbooks, flip through them, nothing.

In the living room, there's a picture of Billy and Kerry on the mantel. They're standing by the fence in front of the roses. Kerry is smiling, holding up a blue ribbon. Billy has his arm around her, looking proud.

There's an album on the shelf. I take it down and open it. Birthday cards. Valentines. Restaurant menus. Letters. "To my dearest Kerry . . ." "To Billy, my only love . . ." I read a few lines here and there. I study the photographs . . . Kerry by a Christmas tree. Billy polishing a boat. Kerry in the kitchen, cooking. Billy holding a humongous lobster. They never had any children. They were each other's whole life. No wonder Billy couldn't bear to be without her.

When I turn the final page, a paper falls out. Yellow lined, folded in half. I open it. There are splotches over some of the words, and it's nearly cracking in the middle, like it's been opened and refolded many times.

"Kerry Blye's Secret Recipe."

For the best tasting chowda in the state of Massachusetts.

I read down the list of ingredients—potatoes, clams . . . all common stuff . . . until I get to the last ingredient. And then I smile.

Now it makes sense.

It's late when I get home. I lost track of time looking through the album. I race up to the attic. "Nanbull! I've got a really colorful detail!"

"I'm sorry, Kip," she says, "we missed the deadline."

"No, it has to be in tomorrow morning's paper."

"It won't run now until Saturday," Nanbull says.

"But Blye's funeral is tomorrow. It has to run tomorrow."

"That's impossible, Kip. The paper's already gone to press and—"

"Billy can't go until his truth is told! Everybody in Clover has to know."

My body is shaking like a blender.

Nanbull's eyes are popping out. "Then tell them yourself tonight at the wake."

CHAPTER 18

"Calling All Clover"

Ride on!
Rough-shod if need be,
smooth-shod if that will do,
but ride on!
Ride on over all obstacles,
and win the race!

—Charles Dickens, *David Copperfield*

But what if nobody comes to Billy Blye's wake? I think about the turnout for Abe Banfield. Only four people came.

Billy needs to lose that anchor so he can sail tomorrow.

How can I get Clover to come to Campbells tonight?

I bike fast to Tuck's house.

"Wait till ya hear this, Kip," he says. "That four-leaf clover you gave me worked. Dad wasn't mad at all about us breaking into Billy Blye's. He said Blye never would say where he caught all those lobsters. Even when he retired, he wouldn't tell. And, look, my dad gave us these battery lamps for Guts. He's getting new ones for the boat."

"That's great, Tuck, but listen." I tell him how we need to get lots of people to Billy Blye's wake tonight.

"Why? Who cares about—"

"It's important, Tuck."

"Is it tied to the million dollars?"

"Well, yeah . . . long term," I say. I think about how I haven't eaten all day. Probably lost the two pounds I gained.

We bike to Jupey's. We tell him what we've got to do. He studies our faces. He's got good poker sense, Jupe does. He doesn't waste time asking for explanations. His dad's in the business. When there's an "APB," all points bulletin, every second counts.

"I'm in," he says.

Biking to Stew's, Jupey cups his fist around his mouth like he's talking through a police megaphone, joking, "A-P-B . . . A-P-B . . . calling all Clover, calling all Clover . . . report to Campbell and Sons

Funeral Home tonight at seven o'clock."

It's warm inside the Bumblebee. Mrs. Brumbaugh smiles when she sees us.

"Mrs. Bee," I say, "Will you to come to Campbell's tonight, for Billy Blye's viewing? We really need everybody to come."

"Sure thing, Kip," Mrs. Brumbaugh says. "Anything for your family. You go along, Stew. And I'll close up early to come. But can't you take a quick break first, boys? Maybe some chili-cheese fries?"

No problem there. "Load us up, Mrs. Bee."

We shovel in the fries like it's a contest, checking out one another's plates.

"The application for Camp Russell came today," Mrs. B says. "You boys need to sign up early to reserve a spot. Place is getting so popular, kids from all over the country . . ."

I see Stew shake his head at his mom, secretly tilting his head toward Tuck.

Mrs. Bee stops talking when she sees Tuck's face.

"How much is it now?" Tuck asks.

"Six hundred dollars a week," Mrs. Bee says, pouring us some more root beer.

"Not happenin' for me," Tuck says.

"Me, either, Tuck," I say.

*

We divide Clover into fourths and head off to round up as many bodies as we can. Live ones. It doesn't take too long to hit the hotspots. Like I said, if you blink when you sneeze, you could miss us.

Tuck takes Belcher's Bowling and the barbershop.

Jupe covers PriceCheck, the gas station, and the docks.

Stew does the Arcadia, Rubin's Auto, and Paulie's.

My first stop is Walgreen's. Drew Callahan is at the checkout. "Hi, Kip," she says, and then *plumpflumpblumblumblahblahblah* she keeps talking, but it's like bubbles in my ears underwater. For the first time ever, I have trouble hearing.

"Come to Campbells tonight at seven p.m.," I say, and bolt out the door.

At Sal's Sips and Subs, Bub and Dirk are in the front booth, stuffing their faces.

"What are you all excited about, Deadbo?" Bub says, sauce dripping off his chin.

I tell them it's the old lobsterman Billy Blye's wake tonight and everybody in Clover is coming because there's going to be a big announcement, but they aren't invited. I figure this way they'll get the whole Clover Clarions team to show up. The more the merrier.

Sal hands me a meatball sub oozing with cheese. "Complimentary, of course."

"I'm late, Sal. Can you wrap it to go? And make sure you come tonight, okay?"

Sal clears his throat. "Will your grandmother be there?"

Smooth, Sal. "Yes," I say, "and I know she'd be happy to see you, Sal."

I check my watch. Shoot, it's late, but I have one more stop to make.

"No," Birdie shouts when I ask her. "Not in'trested."

"Please, Birdie. You come to every wake, anyway. I've seen you. I work there. I live there. My last name is Campbell. Kip *Campbell*. You know my grandmother, Nora. My dad is the undertaker. The big, tall guy you said was kind to Billy. I know my sister probably spooks you—she's the tall skinny one with the wacky clothes and freaky hair—but I am personally inviting you to come."

"No!" Birdie says. "Go away." She slams the door in my face.

*

I'm nearly home when I think of one more thing. Something I need to get from Billy Blye's place. I race back, heart pounding. The wake is less than an hour away.

It's so dark now it's hard to see, but I find one still blooming.

CHAPTER 19

Billy Blye's Final Show

He'd make a lovely corpse.

—Charles Dickens, *Martin Chuzzlewit*

The lights in the viewing room are low. Just two flower arrangements. One my mother made up this afternoon. The other says "To Uncle." The card reads, "Love, Carla."

I walk slowly toward the casket, take a deep breath, and look.

Uncle Marty did a real nice job on Billy Blye's face. And Aunt Sal was clever about solving the eye problem. She angled Billy's blue captain's cap down on the left side. He's wearing the yellow rain slicker I brought from his cottage.

"Hey there, Cap'n Billy." I look back quick to

make sure we're alone. "I did what you asked me. I got the truth and I'll tell it tonight. But it was an accident, Billy. It wasn't your fault . . ."

"What are you, talking to dead people now?" Lizbreath is breathing over my shoulder. "I thought you were afraid of him. 'Oh mommy, mommy, he took my kite.'"

"Shut up, Lizard." Lizard, new, I like it. The doorbell rings. Dad calls us.

Dad and Mom are in the hallway, talking with a lady I've never seen before.

"Kip . . . Lizbeth," Dad says. "I'd like you to meet Mrs. Hughes. Mr. Blye's niece."

I extend my hand. "I'm sorry for your loss, ma'am." She's pretty for a ma'am.

"Thank you, Kip." She smiles at me. "Call me Carla."

"Let me take your coat, Carla," Lizbeth says. "And I'll show you where the restroom is. If you'd like water or coffee or anything, just let me know. And you'll want to sign the register book first before . . ."

Carla stares past the babbling Lizard into the room where her uncle Billy is laid out. She looks at my father. He offers her his arm. She accepts it, her face crumpling a bit. "It's been ten years, Mr. Campbell, since I've seen him. I didn't think I'd . . ."

"It's okay," Dad says, patting her arm. "Would you like me to go with you?"

"Yes," Carla says. Her face looks grateful.

I watch my father walk Carla over to Billy's coffin.

When she sees her uncle's face, Carla puts her hand to her mouth and makes a squeaking sound. Dad stands behind her at a respectful distance. Carla kneels down.

When she hunches over, shoulders shaking, crying, Dad moves forward and rests his hand on her back. They stay there awhile like that, not talking.

Mom is next to me, watching too. "Your father's so good, isn't he, Kip? Cares so much about people. He was born to be a funeral director."

"Yeah," I say, turning away.

"Kip, wait." Mom locks my eyes with hers. "It's okay if you're not."

"Not what?"

"Born to be a funeral director."

I feel a punch in my gut.

Mom touches my cheek. "Listen to your heart's calling, son. That's the path to follow."

The doorbell rings. Then again and again.

"Clover came through for Billy Blye," I say to Nanbull.

"No," Nanbull says. "Clover came through for *you*. They came because Kip Campbell asked them."

Soon, we have a full house. It's like Remembering Day at Willow Grove. Dad and Mom are surprised.

"I didn't know Billy had so many friends," Mom says.

"We never know how a death will affect us," Dad says.

Aunt Aggie is playing Irish music. "The Rose of Killarney" and "Danny Boy". Stew and Jupey are handling the parking lot for me. Drew Callahan comes with her parents.

Lizard—I love it, *Lizard*—is huffing about having to lug coats upstairs. She is in a nasty mood, a really nasty mood.

Chick, on the other hand, is having a grand time. Sticking smiley faces on people.

Poor Carla looks overwhelmed but happy in a way. All these people coming out to honor her uncle, offering their condolences, shaking her hand.

Everything's going perfect. I'm about to make my announcement. When all of a sudden, I hear Lizard.

"You! What are *you* doing sneaking in here?"

I rush out to the vestibule. "Shut up, Liz. She's my friend."

Birdie O'Shaughnessy is wearing a canary yellow dress, her hair combed nice with a ribbon. She's scrubbing her hands together so fast her yellow pocketbook is bobbing on her arm like a buoy.

"Welcome, Birdie," I say. "I'm glad you came."

"You *know* her?" Lizard says, looking at me, shocked.

Birdie looks nervous as a gull on the beach worrying you'll grab back the crust you tossed. "I should've worn black," Birdie says, looking at my sister.

"You're fine," I say. "You look nice." I offer Birdie my arm.

She grabs on quick. Her arm's like a twig. I lead her into the viewing room.

People stop talking. Everyone stares. Birdie pulls away like she's going to fly.

"It's okay," I whisper. "It's okay."

Chick runs over to us, all excited, like finally the birthday girl came. "Hi, lady!" She pulls on Birdie's yellow dress. Birdie looks down at her.

"Look," Chick says, showing Birdie her sheet of

stickers. "Do you want a red one, a yellow one, a blue, or a green?"

Birdie bends down. She studies the sheet. "You pick one fer me," she says.

"Sure." Chick giggles, all happy that somebody's playing along. "Green."

Birdie nods her head. "Green, that's right. I'm A'rish, ya know," she says.

"Me too," Chick says. "We're neighbors."

Birdie O'Shaughnessy cracks a smile. It's not a pretty sight. Nobody's gonna be calling Birdie to do toothpaste commercials anytime soon.

Chick sticks a green smile on Birdie's wrinkled face. Chick's little finger with the sloppy purple nail polish presses the smile in hard. "Got to make sure it stays."

"Give me another," Birdie says, and Chick doubles over laughing.

Chick peels off another green smiley and sticks it on Birdie's other cheek.

"I like you," Chick says loudly.

Birdie stops smiling. Her lips tremble like she's gonna bawl. She looks over at the coffin. At Billy Blye. A tear runs down her cheek.

I think maybe Birdie O'Shaughnessy liked Billy Blye more than she ever let on.

Chick wraps her arms around Birdie's leg. "Come on," Chick says. She looks up at Birdie with an angel face. "Don't be scared. I'll hold your hand."

My throat squeezes tight as I watch Chick and Birdie walk toward Billy's coffin.

Nanbull whispers in my ear, "Nice work, Kip. You've got a gift."

Father Tallman leads some prayers and then asks if "anyone has a few words."

No one steps forward. No surprise. I wait a second, and then I do.

I tell them Billy's truth, plain and simple. Short and sweet.

Nobody seems shocked. The waves did it. Clearly an accident. No big deal.

It was to me, Kip Campbell, and I thank ya dearly.

And I'm sorry about yer kite. Those were Kerry's roses and . . .

I sewed the kite up for ya, I did, fixed the string, and set it out by the fence, figuring ya'd come back, but the wind must have took it first.

People are talking with Birdie O'Shaughnessy. The lady in the canary yellow dress with the two green smiles on her cheeks. Birdie's own smile makes three.

She's glowing like she's at a prom. Laughing, light and happy, like she's fifty years younger. It makes me feel good to see her that way. She isn't a woodle after all.

I think about the paper cranes hanging in her cottage, how fragile and beautiful they are. Not something you'd expect from a Birdlady.

I wonder what made Birdie hole away like a hermit crab in the first place.

I wonder, did she love Billy Blye? Maybe she hoped he'd pick her?

I guess I'll never know. "People's entitled to their secrets," as Birdie says.

Maybe you can never know what's inside another person. Or what anchors might be weighing them down.

All I know is, it sure feels nice when you can help somebody sail.

When the last of the guests leave, Carla Hughes hugs me. "Thank you, Kip, for your eulogy. It explains so much about the change in my uncle. He was always nice to me when I was little. But after Aunt Kerry's death, he became a different person. Just plain mean. It was scary. I didn't understand. But now I do. Now

I know there was something eating away at him. So much pain and guilt."

I walk Carla out to her car. I tell her about the recipe I found in the album.

"Oh, that's funny," she says. "I'd forgotten. Aunt Kerry's famous chowda recipe. She was always such a nudge about her secret ingredient. What was it anyway?"

I tell her.

"That's strange," Carla says. "That wouldn't have affected the taste. I know because I cook a lot. I love adding flowers. Dandelions. Marigolds. Two tiny rose petals wouldn't make a difference."

"Do you want the recipe?" I say, opening the door of her car.

"Sure," Carla says. "No . . . wait. Give it to that nice woman I met tonight, the one who runs the diner."

"The Bumblebee. That's my friend's, Stew's, mom. Mrs. Brumbaugh."

"Good," Carla says, smiling. "Give her the recipe. It'll be my way of thanking the people of Clover for coming out for Uncle Billy tonight. I have a feeling they wouldn't have come without some coaxing. And I have a feeling I have *you* to thank for that."

She sticks out her hand and we shake.

"No problem," I say. "Anytime. We Campbells are here to serve."

"You have a nice family, Kip," Carla says. "You're lucky. So much love. And nice friends, too. It was good of that one boy to bring flowers."

That was Tuck. He carried in a pot of orange mums, looked like he grabbed them off a neighbor's front stoop. Probably did, but who cares? It's the thought that counts.

"And who was that cute girl you were talking to?" Carla says.

"Nobody. Just someone from school."

Nobody, my gut. Drew Callahan. My face gets red just thinking about her. She snuck me a slip of paper with her screen name: Druelove13. "What are you doing Halloween?" she said. "Maybe we can get together."

It's after midnight, everyone's asleep. I sneak down to the viewing room.

I walk toward the coffin, feeling peaceful inside.

"You're all set now, Billy, go to good. Kerry's waiting on the other shore." I put the rugosa in his hand. "Give her this when you land, captain. Bon voyage."

*

When I turn around, I see my father standing in the doorway.

I walk toward him.

He looks like he wants to ask me something, but he just smiles and pats me on the shoulder. "Long day, son. Let's get some sleep." He shuts off the light.

Meow.

Dad flicks on the light. We turn toward the casket.

Mosely's sitting up in the coffin wearing Billy's cap.

Capt'n Mosely in his tuxedo, looking like he runs a cruise ship.

"Get out of there," Dad says. "You crazy cat."

Meow.

Dad and I crack up laughing.

CHAPTER 20

We're Golden Too

There is a wisdom of the head,
and . . . a wisdom of the heart.

—Charles Dickens, *Hard Times*

The next morning, I sit next to Dad in Black Beauty. Mosely's on his leash on my lap. Mose knows this is a banner day. He's never been in Black Beauty before.

Well, at least not that we know about.

It's a small procession to Willow Grove Cemetery. The willows wave as we drive up the hill. It's a nice day, blue sky, sunny. The wind is perfect for sailing.

Carla Hughes is in the lead limousine behind us, with Mom, Lizbeth, and Chick.

Then Uncle Marty and Aunt Sal.

Father Tallman and Doc Burton.

In the caboose spot, in Gramp's antique hearse, are three spiffy ladies in bright red hats. Nanbull, Aunt Aggie, and Birdie O'Shaughnessy. Aunt Aggie needed convincing about the red hat, but Nanbull said, "Don't be a mouse. Live a little."

After the service, Mom hands Carla a basket with pink hearts drooping down.

"For your garden," Mom whispers with a smile.

When we get home, I take off my black suit, change, and bike to the water.

I start to head out to my throne, but then decide to walk the beach instead. My stomach growls. I forgot to pack lunch. So much has happened in these past few days, I forgot all about gaining weight. I forgot all about the . . .

Something's shining in the sand ahead of me. A glittery pebble. Then another and another. I pick them up.

Gold!

I race to Clover Stamp and Coin.

"Where'd you get these," the guy says.

"On the beach," I say.

The guy goes to the scales. "Two ounces," he says.

Gold is still $590 an ounce. Nearly twelve hundred dollars. It's enough to pay for . . .

I bike home and run upstairs. Mom and Dad are having coffee in the kitchen.

My face is sweaty, my chest is pounding. "Dad, can I please go to Camp Russell with Tuck this sum—"

"Sure."

"*What*?" That was easy.

"We were just talking about it actually," Dad says. "Mrs. Burmbaugh brought over the application. We were about to fill it out."

I rush to hug him. "Thanks, Dad."

Mom winks at me.

Next stop, Wayshak's. Carla Hughes asked if I'd find a good home for Hook.

"Hey, buddy," I say in a soft voice as I carry him out. "Don't be scared." I slide his cage onto my handlebars. "Billy's gone now. He's good."

"*Billygood, Billygood.*"

I laugh. "That's right, buddy. You're smart for a bird."

I keep my hand on the cage so he won't fall off as we ride.

The window is open at Birdie's cottage. As we get close, I can hear her singing.

"When ar-rish I's are smilin', sure 'tis like a morn in spring . . ."

"*Rock-a-bye, rock-a-bye,*" Hook squawks.

The singing stops. Birdie opens the door. "So, yer Hook," she says.

She takes the cage from my hand. Carries it in. Sets it down on the table. "Never had a pet before." She sticks her finger in the cage.

"*Rock-a-bye, rock-a-bye,*" Hook squawks.

Birdie laughs. "Like me singin', do ya?" She pets Hook's head. "Look at you. Good as gold."

I turn to sneak away before she changes her mind.

"Don't be a stranger, Skipper," Birdie says.

"I won't, Birdie. I promise."

Biking to Guts I see a new billboard for Golden's Funeral Home.

"Price. Selection. Service. We've Got the Others Beat."

It sounds like they're talking about buying cars.

It's not about prices. It's about people. Caring about people. Dead and alive.

Golden, huh? Well we're golden, too. The Outdoor Guy has connections.

CHAPTER 21

The Funeral Director's Son

Reflect upon your blessings,
of which every man has many,
not on your past misfortunes,
of which all men have some.

—Charles Dickens

Tuck, Jupe, and Stew are already there when I get to Guts.

Mrs. Bee sent black-and-white cookies, potato knishes, corned beef on rye, a six-pack of orange soda, and a thermos full of chowda. A new recipe.

"And look, Kip," Jupe says. "Five bags of Halloween candy. Dad stocked up early at the station and—"

"Jupey, Stew, listen," I have to blurt it out. "Tuck

and I are coming to Camp Russell next summer."

Tuck stops chewing. "We are? No way. You know I can't afford—"

"My treat," I say.

"No way," Tuck says. "I don't want charity."

"Cut it out, Tuck. This isn't a handout. Consider it an early birthday present. I came into an unexpected inheritance." I turn my back so Stew and Jupe can't see me wink at Tuck. "A one in a *million* opportunity."

"Sweet!" Tuck shouts, coming toward me, fist out to seal the deal.

Someday I'll tell them about the gold. And maybe someday about the voices, but for now . . . food, friends, fun. That's all I'm thinking about today.

We finish the cookies. Dig into the candy. Play some poker.

When it's time to go, Stew says, "r-p-s for the last bag of Skittles."

Paper. Scissors. Rock. For the first time ever, I win.

"Whoa," Jupe says.

"Luck-ee," Tuck says.

Later, I head down to the marina. The sun is setting, the sky is pumpkin orange.

Halloween's coming. Druelove13.

I walk out to a Nauset Whaler. Slide my hand across the hull.

"She's a beauty, huh?" a fisherman shouts over to me. He hauls a net of striped bass up out of his boat and slaps it down wet and wriggling on the dock.

"You're Boss Campbell's boy, aren't you?"

I've never seen him before, must be new in Clover. Already he knows my dad.

"That's right," I say. "I'm Kip Campbell. The funeral director's son."

Acknowledgments

With special thanks to . . .

Rubin Pfeffer, Publisher, Simon & Schuster, for "dreaming big," and my wonderful editors Emily Meehan and Courtney Bongiolatti.

My agents Tracey and Josh Adams of Adams Literary.

My son, Connor, for the firefly night of ideas on Cape Cod and for bringing a certain tuxedo cat, formerly known as Michael, into our family.

My son, Dylan, for the perfect answer to the question: "What do twelve-year-old boys want?" Which at first I dismissed and later realized was golden.

My brother, Jerry Murtagh, for the rainbow candles, which sparked the first draft of this novel, and to Noreen, Michael, Danny, and Kevin, siblings extraordinaire.

Thanks also to . . .

The many fine funeral service professionals with whom I had the pleasure of working during my affiliation with the Dodge Company of Cambridge, Massachusetts, especially Jake and Mike Dodge, Kristen Frederick, Frank Connelly, John Cannon, John Clinton, Bill Leahy, Anthony Amigone, Jim Dean, Mark Levine, Mark Anthony, Bill McVeigh, and Ellen McNulty.

My friend forever in spirit, Mari-Beth Moore Barrett, who inspired the *Remembering Book*, a way to celebrate the stories of the people we love.

My mother, Peg Spain Murtagh, my greatest teacher.

You are all golden in my book.

C. M. P.

MYSTERY. ADVENTURE. HOMEWORK.
Enter the World of Dan Gutman.

Getting Air
978-0-689-87681-3

Nightmare at
the Book Fair
978-1-4169-2438-8

The Homework Machine
978-0-689-87679-0

Back in Time with
Thomas Edison
978-0-689-84125-5

Back in Time with
Benjamin Franklin
978-0-689-87884-8

Published by Simon & Schuster
Books for Young Readers